WHEN *Goodbye* IS ALL YOU HAVE

WHEN *Goodbye* IS ALL YOU HAVE

A Novel

TRINITY SIERRA SESAY

Publisher's Cataloging-in-Publication

Sesay, Trinity Sierra.
    When goodbye is all you have / Trinity Sierra Sesay. -- Durham, North Carolina : By Vanessa S. LLC, [2025]
    272 pages ; 21 cm.
    ISBN 979-8-9923993-8-7 (paperback)
    LCCN 2025913232

    I. Title.
    1. African American women--Fiction. 2. Romance fiction, American.
    3. Interpersonal relations--Fiction. 813'.6—dc23

DEDICATION

For the hearts that learned to rest in the endings they didn't choose.

CHAPTER ONE

Symeria

The restaurant was dimly lit, the air thick with the scent of rosemary and seared meat. A soft hum of conversation surrounded her, couples leaning in close, sharing quiet laughter, wine glasses clinking in a celebratory rhythm. The warmth of candlelight flickered against the polished mahogany tables, giving the space an almost romantic glow.

She stood near the entrance, clutching her purse, eyes scanning the room for… something… someone.

A man dressed in a crisp white shirt and black vest stepped forward, menu in hand, his voice smooth but firm as he called out, "Hayes, party of one?"

Symeria blinked, her chest tightening.

She glanced around, suddenly aware of the pairs of eyes flickering toward her. Some were quick and dismissive, others lingering with silent questions.

Party of one.

The words echoed, carrying an unfamiliar weight as the host repeated himself, louder this time, "Hayes, party of one!"

The statement stretched, warped, morphing into something deeper than just a dinner arrangement. It was a reminder. A confirmation.

She was alone.

Her feet felt like lead, and her voice caught somewhere between protest and silence.

Before she could move, the scene around her shifted. The voices dimmed, the restaurant fading into a blur of candlelight and whispered conversations. She was the only thing left in focus.

Alone.

Her chest heaved, but before she could fully react, she woke up.

❦

7:15 AM.

Thirty minutes to get dressed. Fifteen to make it to the office.

People assumed being the CEO meant setting her own hours, but the reality was the opposite—especially when running one of the fastest-growing technical training companies in Georgia. The early morning meetings were non-ne-

Trinity Sierra Sesay

gotiable, but Symeria was seriously considering hiring a new assistant. One who understood the meaning of scheduling after nine.

She exhaled deeply, stepping into the steaming shower. The heat wrapped around her, momentarily melting away the stress. Her almond butter body wash filled the air, grounding her in the moment.

It would've been nice to share mornings like this with someone…

She brushed the thought away. *No time for wishful thinking.*

Twenty minutes left.

She towel-dried quickly, scanning her closet for something work-appropriate that wouldn't leave her sweating by noon. Savannah's June heat was relentless. Her hand landed on a peach-colored Levenity sundress with mint-green floral accents—light, breezy, perfect.

She slipped on her mint-green Coach sandals, swiped on minimal makeup, and ran her fingers through her hair, catching sight of a single gray strand at her temple. A reminder that thirty-five was knocking louder than she liked.

She ignored it, grabbed her orange juice, swallowed her blood pressure pill, and headed out.

—⚬⚬⚬—

"Good morning, Miss Hayes."

"Morning, Darenda. Are they here yet?" Symeria asked, stepping into her office.

"Not yet. Mr. Leonard called and said they're running a little late."

She pinched the bridge of her nose. "How late?"

"He didn't say."

"If they're more than fifteen minutes behind, reschedule them. And remind him that this is a professional establishment. We don't do late."

Darenda hesitated. "LATE, Miss Hayes?"

"Late Arrivals, Darenda."

She nodded, scribbling something down.

Symeria sighed and sank into her leather executive chair, swiveling toward the window. A year ago, this was just a dream: her own company, her own rules.

She remembered the night she announced it to her parents.

Her dad had been watching reruns of *Hawaii 5-0*, his usual addiction, when she blurted out, "I have an announcement."

Without looking up, her mom quipped, "What? You're getting married?"

Symeria snorted. "To do that, Ma, I'd need a man."

          Trinity Sierra Sesay

They laughed, but when she told them she was starting her own business, the mood shifted. Her dad finally muted the TV.

"You sure?"

"Positive."

When she said *technical training*, her mom got it immediately. The parents supported her from that moment on.

Her friends, on the other hand? Not so much. They thought she was crazy for leaving a six-figure job to go solo. But standing in her office now, she knew she had made the right choice.

The intercom buzzed.

"Miss Hayes, I rescheduled Mr. Leonard."

"Good."

"Oh, and Miss Hayes… you have a call on line one. Mrs. Lewis-Conteh."

Symeria frowned. "This early?" She picked up. "Everything okay?"

"Girl, I'm fine. What about you?"

She smirked. "Shouldn't you be in court, separating happy couples?"

Mrs. Lewis-Conteh giggled. "Nope. Playing hooky today. No divorces, no breakups. Just me, myself, and self-care."

Sye leaned back. "Hooky? You?"

"Listen, last week, I tried to finalize a divorce for a couple who changed their minds at the last minute. I need a break."

"I hear you."

Sye's phone chimed—a text from Torrie. It was a flyer for a new spa.

"So… that's where you're going?"

"Yep. And I want you to come with me."

She laughed. "Torrie, you know I have work."

"What good is having your own company if you can't play hooky once in a while?"

Taureen was baiting her, and it was working. Freedom was her weakness.

She sighed. "Fine. Let me wrap up a few things. What time?"

"Eleven. See you there, boss lady."

She hung up, shaking her head. A spontaneous spa day wasn't on her schedule, but maybe it should be.

CHAPTER TWO

Taureen

Taureen "Torrie" sat at the window seat in her country-style kitchen, nursing a throbbing headache. This was her favorite spot to steal a quiet moment for herself. Something about the white-paneled storage drawers and the big yellow pillows with sunflower designs put her at ease.

Not everything was about work, and she wished she could drill that into Sye's head, but the woman was stubborn. *It's what has gotten her this far.* Torrie had thought she was crazy for leaving her high-powered job at The Training Company when mega-corporations sought her expertise nationwide.

But she did it anyway.

And she succeeded.

Some people knew exactly what they wanted and went after it. Then there were people like Torrie, those who followed the advice of others, chasing what looked good on paper.

"Torrie!"

She snapped out of her daze.

"Huh? What?"

"What were you thinking about?" Amari asked, placing his coffee mug by the sink.

"Oh, nothing really. Just thinking."

"Well, whatever, or should I say, *whoever*, it was must have been interesting."

Torrie rolled her eyes. "What's with this *whoever* nonsense, Amari?"

"I'm just saying that you were lost in thought. If it wasn't me, then maybe it was someone else." His tone was laced with something she didn't have the energy for.

The headache spread, and all she wanted was for him to stop talking. She wasn't in the mood to argue. Lately, that was all they did.

"Do you want me to fix you something to eat?" she asked, hoping to shift the energy.

"Nope. I'm good," Amari responded curtly.

Torrie's jaw clenched, her new habit to keep herself from snapping. She knew he was hungry. He just refused to admit it.

Taking a deep breath, she poured a fresh cup of coffee and placed it on the table.

 Trinity Sierra Sesay

"Do you want to do something today? Hang out? Talk? Just… something?" Her voice came out too bright, too forced. She just wanted to break this coldness between them.

Amari rubbed his chin, pretending to ponder. "Was that question for *me*?" he asked mockingly. "Go out? Do something with *you*? You're asking *me* that?"

"Yes, Amari. I'm asking my husband if he wants to spend time with me." She smiled, hoping it would soften him.

"Oh. *Your husband?*" He let out a bitter laugh. "You mean *me*?" He pointed at himself. "Thanks for remembering your husband." He used air quotes. "But no, I'm good. Besides, wouldn't you rather spend time with your lover? You know, the one you cheated on me with?"

Torrie's patience snapped. "Amari, don't you think this conversation is getting tired?"

"No, Torrie, I don't."

"Well, I do. I'm sick of it."

"That's too bad. Because I wasn't the one who cheated. That was you. I wasn't the one sneaking around town with another man. That was you. So if you're tired of the conversation, maybe you should've made a different choice."

"What do you want from me?" she burst out. "I apologized. I told you it was a mistake and that I would never do it again. Why can't we move on?"

"Move on?" He let out a disbelieving scoff. "How am I supposed to do that? Every time I see you, I think about you and him. Every time I touch you, I think about him touching you first. I can't even kiss you without feeling like my lips are touching his leftovers. And I'm supposed to just *move on?*"

Torrie inhaled sharply. "It's been three months, Amari. It's time to let it go."

"You let it go, Torrie. I'll heal when I'm good and damn ready."

The door slammed behind him as he climbed into his gold Lexus RX and sped off.

Torrie just shook her head, exhaling heavily. *What in the world was I thinking? Is there ever going to be an end to this?*

⧈

By 11 o'clock, Torrie was in the parking lot, waiting for Symeria. The fight with Amari had almost made her cancel, but when she saw Symeria's car pull up, it was too late to back out.

She took a deep breath, put on her best poker face, and practiced her smile in the mirror before stepping out.

"Hey, girl," she greeted, pulling Symeria into a big hug.

"Oooh, what was that for?" Symeria asked, laughing.

"Just for being you."

"Oh really? Well, I need to be me more often. Maybe then I could get hugs like that from men."

They both laughed as they headed inside.

"Can I help you ladies today?" the receptionist, a trendy Black woman with naturally curly hair, greeted them with a warm smile. Torrie suspected she was a little older than them, but her flawless skin and hourglass shape made it hard to tell.

"Yes, we have an eleven o'clock appointment. Conteh and Hayes," Torrie said.

The receptionist checked the schedule. "Got it. And what will you have today, Mrs. Conteh?"

"Everything. Whatever you've got, I want it."

"And you, Mrs. Hayes?"

Symeria cleared her throat. "It's *Miss* Hayes. And I'll have the same."

The receptionist nodded. "Alright then. Follow me."

⸙

Once settled into their spa treatments, Torrie eased into the mud bath beside Symeria, who was already adjusting to the idea of it. Considering how hesitant she'd been about putting her body into what she called *wet dirt*, it was amusing.

"You know," Symeria admitted, "soaking in this mud isn't as bad as I thought."

Torrie rolled her eyes. "Told you. It's actually relaxing. Almost makes me forget how stressed out I've been."

"Those divorcing clients got you frazzled?" Symeria teased.

"No, it's not the clients."

"Then who?"

Torrie hesitated, then met her friend's gaze. "Amari."

Symeria frowned. "What's going on?"

Torrie exhaled heavily. "He found out about my affair with Jarrod. And he just can't get over it."

Symeria stiffened. "Your what? How? When?"

Torrie braced herself, relieved that Symeria wasn't freaking out. She tilted her head back, feeling the mud shift around her, making her suddenly feel trapped. Tears pricked her eyes, but she willed them back.

"It was a mistake," she whispered. "I should've never done it."

Symeria's voice was gentle but firm. "Torrie, talk to me. What happened?"

CHAPTER THREE

Amari

"Get over it."

The words still echoed in his ears, taunting him like a ghost he couldn't shake. Amari clenched his jaw, gripping the steering wheel as his knuckles whitened.

Get over it?

How the hell was he supposed to just move past the fact that another man had been with his wife? She actually had the nerve to say that to his face, like he was supposed to just swallow it down and keep moving.

His stomach twisted. He gritted his teeth so hard it hurt.

Another man had touched what was his. And she wanted him to forget?

Hell no.

The whole thing felt upside down. He knew it was messed up, maybe even unfair, but deep down, he had always assumed that if anyone stepped out, it would be him.

It wasn't right.

But it was real.

He was a card-carrying national life member of the Purple and Gold. They lay it down and bark it out. He was the big man on campus. And she... she was just Torrie.

Or at least, she had been.

When he met her, she was scattered, floating through life without direction. One week she wanted to be a psychiatrist, the next, an engineer. She had no plan. No solid ground. He gave her stability. He gave her time to figure it out.

"I want to be a caterer," she had told him once.

"How can you be a caterer when you can't even cook?" he'd shot back.

"I'll learn."

And that was it. That was what he had to endure. But he stuck it out. He put up with the trial-and-error dishes. The ridiculous business ideas. The expensive dreams. He invested in her before she was anything.

Because let's be real, when he met her, she wasn't much. She was book-smart, yeah, but she wasn't the kind of girl that turned heads. She didn't have the confidence, the polish. She didn't carry herself like the women he was used to at Madison St. U.

But now?

     Trinity Sierra Sesay

Now, she was fine as hell. She dressed well. She walked like she owned the ground beneath her. That body? That ass?

Lord, that ass.

And now that she had grown into herself, now that she was an attorney with prestige and power, every dude on the block wanted to step to her.

What they didn't seem to realize was that *he* made her. *He* shaped her into the woman she had become.

Not them.
Him.

He had supported her financially, emotionally, spiritually, and mentally. If it weren't for him, she'd still be out here trying to figure herself out.

That was what she needed to understand.

So no.
He wasn't just going to forget it.
Ever.

CHAPTER FOUR

Symeria

"Let me get this straight—you had an affair three months ago with Jarrod? Jarrod, the probation and parole officer?"

Torrie shook her head slowly, like even admitting it pained her.

"And Amari found out when he showed up at your office?"

"Yep."

"What gave it away?"

"The flowers," Torrie muttered, burying her face in her hands. She groaned as the mud from the spa treatment smeared across her forehead.

Symeria frowned. "Wait. Flowers? Why would that tip him off? Don't clients send you flowers all the time?"

"Yes, but the card, Sye. The damn card was right next to them. It said, *You were wonderful last night.*"

"Ah. Yeah. That would do it."

Torrie sank lower into the bath, letting out a long sigh.

"Okay, so that was three months ago. You guys are trying to work things out, right?"

"Yes and no. Pastor Allen advised us not to involve other people—he said we'd just get outside opinions messing with our heads. So we didn't. That's why I didn't tell you," she exhaled sharply. "But we're going in circles. He doesn't trust me, and he doesn't want to trust me. He holds onto it like he enjoys this version of us, where I'm always guilty and he's the victim."

"Torrie, I don't think he's happy. It sounds more like he's still hurting."

"Yeah, well, hurt is supposed to heal. He's not healing. If anything, he's getting worse. Every argument, every conversation, he finds a way to bring it up."

Symeria considered that for a moment, soaking in everything she'd just heard. She hadn't even noticed what was happening. No signs. No warnings.

"It's weird, though," she finally said. "He doesn't act like anything is wrong around me. I mean, you would think he'd feel awkward knowing I might know."

"No, he wouldn't. He knew you didn't know. I promised him I hadn't told you."

Sye reached for her hand. "I just hope you two find a way to pick up the pieces."

     Trinity Sierra Sesay

Torrie blinked back tears and exhaled sharply. "Well, enough of that. What do you have planned for the weekend?"

Sye wanted to press her for more but let it go. "The weekend?"

"Yes, the weekend. You know, Friday night, Saturday?"

"Oh, that." She shrugged. "Hot date with a laptop and a spreadsheet."

Torrie let out a dramatic sigh. "Why do you do this? Why do you spend every weekend working? You have to play at some point. When do the games begin?"

"And who am I supposed to play with, Torrie?"

"There are men out there, Sye. You just have to find them."

"*Find* them?" She let out a laugh. "Yeah, okay."

"Seriously, Sye. You're not going to meet anyone holed up in your den watching *Hawaii 5-0* with your laptop on your legs."

"Really? Because Chin Ho Kelly is fine," Sye smirked, expecting her to laugh, but she just stared, unimpressed. "I see you're not amused."

"Look, I get it. But we've had this conversation before. You don't meet men because you don't put yourself out there. And when you do meet someone, they're either married, attached, or carrying enough baggage to sink a cruise ship. Maybe, just maybe, your standards are a tad too high?" She held up her fingers an inch apart.

"Standards are a guide, that's all. Some things I can be flexible on, but some things I won't tolerate. Either way, it doesn't matter if I don't even have opportunities to meet anyone."

Torrie's lawyer brain was working—Sye could tell. She was trying to fix what she saw as a problem, and God, it was annoying.

"Have you tried online dating?" she asked.

Sye groaned. "Online dating? You want me to wade into that cesspool?"

"It's 2024, Sye. Everyone's doing it. Just set up a profile and bam—instant options. There are plenty of eligible bachelors out there, probably just like you."

"You know what else can happen? I could go missing or end up in a *Dateline* special. So no, I haven't tried it, and I'm not going to. I'm not that desperate."

"You said it yourself. The issue isn't you—it's that you don't meet anyone. You haven't seriously dated since Lindsey."

"And I'm good with that."

"Okay, suit yourself," she shrugged. "Just remember, I tried."

"I know you did. And thanks. But when Mr. Wonderful shows up, it won't be through a dating app."

The conversation drifted from her nonexistent dating life to Torrie's latest client crisis. By the time they finished their

 Trinity Sierra Sesay

spa treatments, Sye felt lighter, like they had massaged the stress right out of her.

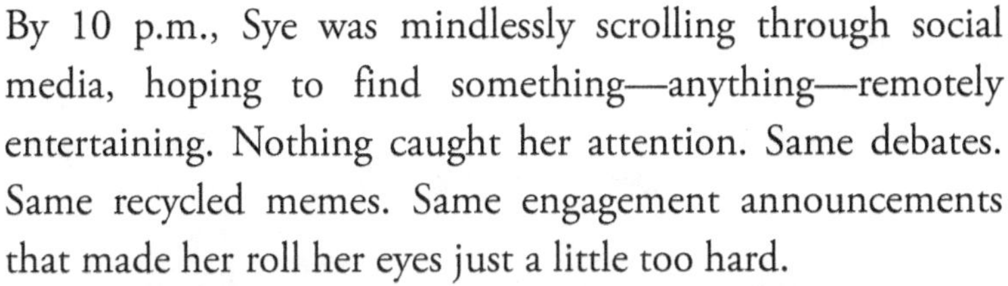

Later that evening, Sye swung by the office to grab her laptop. As she turned the last corner, she nearly ran into Darenda.

"Oh, Miss Hayes, I wasn't expecting you back. I was just about to lock up."

"That's fine, Darenda. I just need to grab my laptop."

Darenda laughed. "Your laptop? Who takes work home on a weekend?"

Sye gave her a pointed look. "Maybe people who actually do work, Darenda."

She straightened immediately, clearly realizing she'd misstepped. "Well, have a great weekend, Miss Hayes."

"You too. See you on Monday."

By 10 p.m., Sye was mindlessly scrolling through social media, hoping to find something—anything—remotely entertaining. Nothing caught her attention. Same debates. Same recycled memes. Same engagement announcements that made her roll her eyes just a little too hard.

Bored, she tapped on a link someone in her Facebook group had shared earlier. A dating site they swore by. She hesitated for a beat, her thumb hovering over the screen.

She wasn't the online dating type. Torrie had brought it up before, but she'd dismissed it. Swiping through strangers, trying to decode who was normal and who was a walking red flag? No, thank you.

Still... she clicked.

The homepage was sleek and inviting, filled with pictures of smiling couples and bold promises about meaningful connections. She scoffed but kept scrolling.

Find your perfect match today.

"Uh-huh, sure," she muttered, but she tapped *Sign Up* anyway.

As the profile setup loaded, she told herself this was just for fun. Just to see what was out there. Nothing serious.

First Name: Symeria

Username: EveAfterDark

She smirked. Something about it felt mysterious. Alluring.

Next were the basics—age, location, and interests. She kept it simple, but when it asked for a bio, she paused.

The best connections start with being vulnerable about what makes you you.

She sighed. Vulnerable? On the internet? That was asking a lot.

After a moment of thought, she typed:

I believe in good conversations, great food, and laughter that lingers long after the joke is over. I'm here for genuine connections, not small talk that leads nowhere. Tell me something interesting, and I just might reply.

Not too much. Not too little. Just enough.

She uploaded a picture with a soft smile—nothing too forced—and hit *Save.*

The second she did, her stomach flipped.

She locked her phone and tossed it onto the nightstand charger.

Maybe this was a mistake. Maybe I'll delete it in the morning.

But as she settled under the covers, a small part of her wondered...

What if it wasn't?

A few minutes later, she reached over, grabbed her phone from the nightstand, and unlocked it. She opened the app again.

To her surprise, something of interest stood out in bold: NextLevelNate — Member of the Week.

He was cute, Sye admitted. She clicked on his profile.

5'9", single, no kids. Scorpio.

At the bottom, his occupation read: *Unemployed.*

She sighed. "Knew there'd be a catch."

Just below, his profile read: *If you enjoy deep convos under the stars, hit me up.*

"Yeah, right. I doubt you even know how to spell 'conversations,' bro."

She was about to close the app, but something made her hesitate. It was harmless entertainment. No one would know.

So why not?

She narrowed her search filters: Ages 35–42. African American. College graduate. Single.

Seventy-nine matches popped up.

Most were uninspiring, but one caught her eye: JayInMotion.

Tan complexion. Deep brown, almond-shaped eyes. A smile framed by a neatly trimmed goatee.

Her fingers hovered over the inbox.

Should I?

She sighed and typed:

Hey, JayInMotion. I came across your profile and thought you seemed interesting. Looking for a friend?

She cringed at how corny it sounded, but she hit send anyway.

No turning back now.

CHAPTER FIVE

Taureen

"Amari!" Torrie yelled, stepping out of the bedroom. "Amari, is that you?"

"Yeah," he called back, his voice carrying up the staircase. "It's me."

She descended a few steps, arms crossed. "It's two-thirty in the morning, Amari. Where the hell have you been?"

He stood at the foot of the stairs, his expression unreadable. "What's with the third degree? Why are you questioning me like I'm some damn teenager? I'm grown, Taureen. I don't need permission to hang out if I choose to. Besides..." His gaze traveled down her body, lingering before he smirked. "Judging by the way you're dressed, you weren't exactly waiting up for me anyway."

Torrie's stomach twisted. She glanced down at the lavender lace teddy she had slipped into earlier for him. She had chosen it because it was seductive but classy, revealing but not desperate. And, of course, it was his favorite color. Purple. It didn't even matter that it was two shades lighter than the brotherhood's signature hue—he always said any purple was close enough.

But now, looking at the way Amari regarded her, she felt exposed in a way she hadn't intended.

"What do you mean, judging by the way I'm dressed?" she demanded. "Purple is your favorite color. I was wearing this for you."

Amari let out a short, bitter laugh as he climbed the stairs. "For... me?" He tapped his chest mockingly. "Come on, Taureen. You really expect me to believe that? The only reason it's for me," he tapped his chest again, harder this time, "is because I'm the only one here right now."

Her throat tightened. "How dare you talk to me like that? I wore this tonight because I wanted to be with you. My husband. I wanted us to reconnect, talk, make love." Her voice broke slightly, but she pushed forward. "I am trying to fix this marriage, Amari. And it feels like I'm the only one even trying."

He paused at the top of the stairs, looking at her, taking her in. And for a moment, just a moment, she thought she saw something crack beneath his hard exterior.

But then his expression shifted again. Cool. Unreadable.

"Taureen," he said, voice controlled and measured, "maybe you're the only one trying... because you're the only one who broke this marriage in the first place. Ever thought about that?"

     Trinity Sierra Sesay

He let the words settle before shaking his head.

"You're a divorce lawyer, right? Then let's be real about this. You said you wanted to talk? Let's talk."

He strode past her into the bedroom and dropped onto the edge of the bed, hands clasped between his knees as he looked up at her.

"Fact," Amari said, his voice low but firm, "you had an affair. Fact. Even after I found out, you kept seeing him. Fact. You lied about it for months. And the real kicker?" He let out a dry laugh. "You never once gave me a real explanation. That whole 'I was lonely, and I needed attention' excuse? Bullshit. You had attention. You had me. So tell me, Taureen," he spread his arms wide, "since you really want to talk, talk. Why? Why did you do it?"

Torrie felt cornered, like the walls were closing in. After four weeks of therapy, he still didn't understand. Hadn't he listened? Hadn't she told him? Hadn't she explained?

Maybe not clearly enough. Maybe he just couldn't accept it. Maybe... maybe I just need to try one more time.

She inhaled deeply. "Amari, I know I told you this, but it seems like you just don't understand."

His eyes narrowed. "Oh, I don't?" His voice dripped sarcasm as he gestured wildly.

She steadied herself. "As I told you before," she took a step forward, her voice slow, deliberate, "I love you, Amari. I always have. But I needed more. Sexually." She enunciated the word, making sure to drive it home. "I wanted to explore. I wanted to experience more. I wanted to try different things, but you didn't. And at some point, it felt like you didn't even want me at all."

She expected a reaction. Some sign that he heard her. That something clicked.

Instead, his face twisted into something colder than anger: disgust.

Amari pushed up from the bed, shaking his head. "So basically, what you're telling me... is that you wanted to be a hoe?"

The words struck like a slap.

He didn't wait for her response. He just turned and walked out of the room.

Torrie closed her eyes, inhaled sharply, and let out a slow, shaking breath.

Never in her life had words from her own husband hurt her so much.

CHAPTER SIX

Symeria

The shrill ring of Sye's phone cut through the quiet, yanking her out of sleep. She groaned, rolling over to glare at the green fluorescent numbers on her clock. 7:30 a.m. on a Saturday. This better be good.

She grabbed her phone, answering in her best *why the hell are you calling me this early* voice.

"Hello?"

"What's up, girl? Wake your tired behind up. You know the deal."

The familiar voice made her smile despite her irritation. "DASH!" she practically sang into the receiver. "What's up, girl?"

"Oh, nothing. Just thought I'd check on my sistah, that's all. So how you doin'?" Her voice had the perfect mix of country and ghetto. It always made Sye laugh. It was her signature, especially when she imitated ShaNaNay from *Martin*.

"Where are you?" Sye asked, suddenly alert.

"Still in New York, why? You act like you can't wait to see me or something."

They both laughed.

"Oh please, no one is checking for you like that," Sye teased. "I have better things to do with my time."

"Uh-huh, sure you do. Anyway, I should be there by the end of next week. I'm almost done clearing out."

"Clearing?"

"Yeah. When you leave the military, there's a process called clearing. It takes about two weeks. But I'm almost finished, so I'll be home soon."

"Okay," Sye said, nodding to herself. "Guess I'll figure out everything else later."

Dash picked up on her hesitation immediately. "What's on your mind?"

"Nothing. Just... nothing."

"Mmhmm. Okay. Go ahead and say it: *I'm proud of you, Dash. I wuv you!*" she threw in her best Bugs Bunny impression.

Sye laughed. "You are so stupid. If I didn't know it before, I know it now." Her voice softened. "I *am* proud of you, though. Really. I can't wait to see you."

"Thanks, Sye," she said, her voice momentarily sincere before she flipped the switch. "Okay, that's enough sentimental talk for today. What's going on with you?"

"Same old, same old. The company's doing great. We gained seven new clients this week alone. My receptionist is efficient but gets on my nerves..."

"Hold up, hold up," Dash cut her off. "I asked about you, not your business."

Sye smirked. "I *am* my business."

Dash groaned. "Girl, please tell me you're not working 24/7."

Silence.

"Okay," Dash said dryly. "Enough said."

"What does that mean?"

"Nothing. Just that when I get there, we're gonna discuss this. Savannah has a whole nightlife, a professional crowd, and some fine, healthy men. So, acting like a hermit? Anyway, I don't really know, but I'll find out soon enough."

They both chuckled before Dash added, "Alright, little girl. Gotta go."

"Okay, talk to you later."

Sye hung up and snuggled back under the covers, smiling to herself.

Dash had always been a force of nature. Growing up, she played everything: basketball, volleyball, track, and even cheerleading for two seasons, which was hilarious. She had the voice for it, but she was way too aggressive. Sye was pretty sure the crowd cheered out of fear.

She went straight into the Army after high school while recruiters begged her to play college ball. She always said college was for people who wanted to work, not play. Now she was retiring as a Master Sergeant and, knowing Dash, already plotting her next move.

It was good to hear from her. With that warmth still lingering, Sye pulled the covers over her head and drifted back to sleep.

⸻

By noon, Sye was up and moving around the house. The day was beautiful, one of those picture-perfect Savannah afternoons where the light hit just right, but the air still held that sticky humidity.

Funny how she once hated this city. She used to call it *Slow-vannah* like everyone else, swearing she'd never move back. There was nothing to do: no NBA team and no big-city excitement. The biggest attraction was Tybee Island, and even that got old fast.

Now? She appreciated the stillness.

I don't need clubs or wild nights. I have work, an occasional church service, and my quiet home with this room: my favorite.

  Trinity Sierra Sesay

The office was filled with light from massive French windows. The pastel peach walls, the antique white crown molding, and the splattered paint-effect borders—it was a space designed for peace. The kind of place that made you breathe.

And for Sye, it was a place to think.

Or work.

Sye sighed and decided to get some tasks done, but her stomach interrupted her with a growl.

Cereal sounds like a plan.

She grabbed a bowl and ate quickly before sitting at her desk, sorting through emails. One hundred and forty-four messages. Mostly junk.

As she deleted them, her phone vibrated. A notification from the dating app.

Oh, right. That.

She clicked the message.

<hr>

Dear EveAfterDark,

Hey, thanks for reaching out. I was pleasantly surprised; good surprises are rare these days. I'd love another friend. You can never have too many. I didn't see a profile for you, so I don't know where to start, but here's a little about me.

My name is Aaron. I live in Rincon, GA. I'm an Aeronautical Engineer. Divorced, three kids (11, 9, and 7; they're my pride and joy). I love sports, music, and movies. Sci-Fi is my thing. Just finished watching *The Matrix* for the 50th time. Looking forward to hearing from you.

—JayInMotion

She leaned back in her chair, rereading the message.

So, he lives in Rincon. Country, meaning he likes open space. Works at Gulfstream. Stable job. Three kids? Enough said.

She chuckled to herself, debating whether to respond. Just as she started typing, her doorbell rang.

She wasn't expecting anyone.

Peeking out the window, she spotted a teal green Acura in the driveway.

"Girl, hurry up and open this door! I have to pee!"

She laughed. "For an attorney, you're so damn ghetto."

Torrie grinned as she pushed past her, heading straight for the bathroom. "Shoot, girl. Attorneys have to pee too."

When she came back, she flopped onto the couch. "What are you up to?"

"Just working."

She groaned. "Of course you are. You are your biggest problem."

Sye smirked. "So, what brings you here?"

"Nothing, really. I was heading to the mall, saw your exit, and figured I'd swing by. Thought you might want to roll with the big dog today."

"Tempting. But honestly, I don't even feel like putting on clothes."

"I feel that," she admitted. "But I also needed to get out. Amari's been a jackass."

Sye frowned. "Again?"

"Girl, he called me a hoe last night. Can you believe it? A hoe."

Her eyebrows shot up. "What?! Why?"

"Because I told him why I had the affair for the hundredth time. He just refuses to accept that he wasn't satisfying me."

Sye exhaled, shaking her head. "Torrie, what are you going to do?"

Before she could answer, her phone buzzed again. Another message from Aaron.

Torrie smirked. "And who is that?"

She groaned. "It's nothing. Just a message from some guy on the dating site."

Torrie gasped dramatically. "Oh, we need to talk. Spill. Now."

CHAPTER SEVEN

Dash

Dash was running late, and she knew Denise would straight-up fight if she missed her hair appointment. She hurried outside, waving down a yellow cab. As soon as it pulled up, she slid into the back seat, barely catching her breath.

"816 W. 133rd Street," she said, urgency in her voice.

The driver, a dark-skinned man with chiseled features and a thick African accent, glanced at her through the rearview mirror. "Would you like to take the scenic route or the Hudson?"

"Whichever is fastest. I have fifteen minutes to get there, and I cannot be late."

The driver nodded and took off, weaving through the busy streets. Dash exhaled, letting her head rest against the cool glass window. Tonight was big—her last soiree in New York, her farewell to the military.

Twenty years. Some said time flew, but for her, it was every bit of twenty. She had entered the Army in 2004, fresh out of high school, a private with no rank and an attitude to match. Now, she was retiring as an E8 Master Sergeant. Still with an attitude to match.

But was it all worth it? The sacrifices, the missed holidays, the deployments? She wasn't sure.

The cab jolted to a stop, snapping her out of her thoughts.

"That will be $13.50."

Dash handed the driver a twenty. "Keep the change."

He nodded in appreciation as she stepped out into the warm New York breeze.

Before she even made it inside, a familiar voice called out.

"It's about time you got here, Ms. Dash!" Denise's voice cried across the salon. "Just because you're retiring doesn't mean you get to grace my establishment with your lateness!"

Dash smirked, making her way past the receptionist. "Sorry, Denise. Time got away from me, and you know how hard it is to catch a cab around here."

A few of the women in the salon chuckled, waking an elderly lady who had dozed off under the dryer.

Denise, the owner of The Natural Hair Affair New York, was the only person Dash trusted with her hair. The salon had a modern but Afrocentric feel, with vibrant murals covering

Trinity Sierra Sesay

the walls and R&B humming softly through the speakers. It was a sanctuary.

Denise, standing at her usual post by the mirror, eyed Dash with amusement. "What are we doing today? And don't give me anything crazy."

Dash grinned. "Actually, Denise, I thought I would let you decide. After all, this is the last time you'll be doing my hair. It's my last time in your chair."

Denise gave her a skeptical look, then picked up a bottle of oil sheen from her station. She held it up like a trophy and started mimicking a southern belle.

"Oh, thank you, thank you all for this blessed honor. After three years of toilin' and slavin' on Ms. Dash's hair, I have finally been bestowed this highest honor."

She ended the drama with a makeshift curtsy. By now, everyone in the shop was rolling on the floor, laughing.

Dash shook her head, barely able to talk between laughs. "You are special."

"Yeah," Denise said, "and you were late. Now, sit."

Dash settled into the chair, letting out a small sigh. She was really going to miss this place.

⁂

By the time Denise finished, it was nearly five. Dash had just enough time to rush home, shower, and get dressed before her driver arrived. Everything in this city was a rush—rush here, rush there. She was ready for the slower pace of Savannah.

As she entered her apartment, she noticed a flood of notifications on her phone. Missed calls. Voicemails. Texts.

She sighed, scrolling through and listening to the voicemails as she kicked off her shoes.

Jerome: *Hey Dash, your driver will be there at 7:00 p.m. sharp.*

Eddie: *Dash baby, what's up? Long time no see. I was hoping to catch up with you when I get in town…EDDIE.*

She rolled her eyes and deleted the message.

The next message was from an unknown number.

Hello, Ms. Hayes, this is Audrey Reyeles. I was calling to see if you had a confirmed date for when you plan to move out. I know this is a very hectic time for you, and I just wanted to make sure your departure is a smooth transition. Call me when you receive this. Thank you.

Dash sighed, glancing around her apartment. The thought of packing gave her a headache.

Then came the last message.

Hello Sylena, how are you? It's been a minute or two since we last talked. That's okay. Just wanted to say congratulations and good luck.

Her stomach tightened.

She knew that voice.

Dash tossed her phone onto the bed and closed her eyes.

How did he get my number? And how did he know I was retiring?

The clock read 6:15 p.m., snapping her out of it.

Focus, Dash.

She shook off the unease and hurried to get dressed. This was her night, and she wasn't letting anything ruin it.

⁂

The ballroom erupted into cheers and applause as Dash entered, escorted by a young lieutenant. She hadn't expected to have a driver and arm candy, but there he was—Lt. Godinez, a fine-as-hell MP.

As they approached the head table, Sergeant Major Franklin tapped the microphone.

"Testing, testing… Alright, everyone, please welcome our guest of honor, Master Sergeant Sylena Hayes!"

The applause was thunderous.

Normally, a departing NCO got a simple hail-and-farewell. But this? This was different. These people loved her. This was an all-out celebration.

Sergeant Major Franklin walked over to Dash. "Hayes, you look beautiful. I love that color on you. What's it called?"

"Fuchsia," Dash said in a kid-like manner.

"Yeah, that color," Franklin said, "really looks nice."

Dash eyed the Sergeant Major and smiled, thinking, *Yeah, I know you like this color on me. Actually, he'd like any color on me, including the brown I wear on a daily basis.*

She could see his eyes following the dress from the thin straps at the top, down and around the A-line waist, all the way to the slit on each side of her thighs. Dash knew she was dressed to kill, and the men's reactions confirmed it.

Look at this. All these men gawking at me like I'm an Angus burger.

Just for the fun of it, she walked slowly, giving the onlookers a view of her toned backside. She was never one for bosoms, so she let that go. But between her dress and her body, some happy couple was going to have an argument tonight.

She smiled to herself and took her seat.

⸺ ⚬⚬⚬ ⸺

"Thank you, LT!" Dash yelled as she entered her apartment.

It was well after 3:00 a.m. She glanced at the clock in the living room while pulling off her crystal-colored stilettos.

Whew.

She sighed.

 Trinity Sierra Sesay

Dash laughed as she thought about the activities. Some funny. Some hilarious. Mostly embarrassing. People were funny when they had alcohol in them.

She chuckled again, remembering how SM Franklin was trying to do the Macarena during *DMX's Party Up*. She thought the man was having a spasm. The worst part? He kept doing it and trying to get others to join him. It was a sad state of events.

As Dash removed her clothes and laid them across the bed, the aroma from the White Castle cheeseburgers attacked her with a vengeance. She slipped on a pair of shorts and her favorite NY Knicks sleep shirt and headed toward the kitchen.

That's a damn shame. She smirked. *All that money spent on food, and I decided I wanted a cheeseburger.*

Dash took a glass from the cabinet, rinsed it out, shoved it under the ice machine on the refrigerator, and then poured root beer into the glass. She scooped up the bag of food from the counter and went into the living room.

As she plopped down on the couch and gently placed the glass on the table, she took the remote in her hand and turned on the TV.

This was one of the few things she was ecstatic about when it came to moving—late-night TV, and peace.

No more soldiers.

CHAPTER EIGHT

Symeria

Sye glanced at the clock on her nightstand. 5:30 a.m.

She couldn't believe she was still lying in bed, messaging with a complete stranger.

Her laptop screen cast a dim glow across her sheets as she typed, stifling a laugh.

"You are sooo crazy!" she wrote.

JayInMotion: *"I know, but you're enjoying it. Don't even front."*

"Oh? Aren't we cocky?" she typed back. "You just know I'm enjoying this, huh?"

JayInMotion: *"Absolutely. If you weren't, you would have been asleep hours ago."*

He had a point. She had only been up because she couldn't sleep, planning to binge a new series until she dozed off. She hadn't expected to get sucked into a conversation with Mr. *JayInMotion* himself.

"Speaking of sleep," she wrote, "I really should go. I turn into an unholy mess when I'm exhausted, and I need to find myself in church tomorrow… or should I say, THIS morning?"

JayInMotion: *"Ohhh, so you're one of those Sunday saints? What happens the rest of the week?"*

"That's between me and the Lord!" she replied.

JayInMotion: *"Fair enough. But I really enjoyed this. I hope we can chat again."*

"Yeah… maybe."

A few seconds passed before another message popped up.

JayInMotion: *"EveAfterDark?"*

"Yes?"

JayInMotion: *"This might be a long shot, but… what do you think about moving this conversation beyond the keyboard? Maybe a phone call sometime? You could call me, or I could call you. No pressure."*

She hesitated, her fingers hovering over the keyboard.

"Hmmm, I don't know… I need to think about it."

JayInMotion: "I get it. But hear me out: what's the point of vibing with someone online, having great conversations,

 Trinity Sierra Sesay

and never actually getting to experience them for real? Just a thought."

A winking emoji followed his message, and despite herself, she smiled.

"I hear you. I'll let you know… soon, okay? But for now, get some sleep. And have a good day."

She closed the app and placed her phone on the night-stand, letting out a long breath.

That was a good conversation.

He was funny, easy to talk to, and surprisingly charming. But anyone could be anyone behind a screen.

She turned onto her side, staring at the ceiling.

Was I actually considering this?

CHAPTER NINE

Amari

"Well, don't you look handsome," Torrie said as Amari adjusted the knot in his bow tie.

After two suit changes, he had settled on his tailored gray suit with purple pinstripes, a crisp gold button-down shirt, and a purple-and-gold Kente bow tie—a subtle nod to his fraternity.

"Didn't think you would be up this early for a church service. Must be something special going on."

Amari smirked. "Well, Torrie, as a matter of fact, it is. It's Omega Phi Day at St. Philip's, and since I am an Omega, I figured I'd attend." His voice dripped with sarcasm as he rolled his eyes.

Torrie's expression shifted. "Barbara usually lets me know when you all have a function. I wonder why she didn't call."

"She didn't call because I told her not to," Amari said, meeting her gaze and watching the hurt settle on her face.

"Oh, I see. I wasn't invited." Her voice was steady, but he could see the cracks forming beneath the surface. She carefully set down her coffee cup, almost methodically. "I understand."

She turned and walked out of the kitchen, her back straight, her pace measured. He knew she was saving face. Knew that if she stood there a second longer, she might not be able to hold back the tears he saw glistening in her eyes.

For the first time in a long time, he felt something—anything—beyond anger. Guilt? Maybe. He wasn't sure.

He stood beside the window, staring blankly at the street below, memories flooding in whether he wanted them to or not.

He had gone to surprise her that day. Just a simple lunch date. Something spontaneous. Something thoughtful. He knew they barely had time for each other between their careers, but he was trying.

The flowers on her desk didn't immediately register as a problem. Torrie had plenty of clients who sent gifts. But when Torrie saw him notice them…

That's when he knew.

She tried too hard to play it off. Her body stiffened, her smile tightened, and her eyes darted toward the card as if willing it to disappear before he saw it.

But he saw it.

You were wonderful last night.

Two lines. Simple. Damning.

Last night.

She was supposed to have been at Sye's house, working on contracts. It wasn't unusual. They were best friends, always helping each other out. He had no reason to question it. No reason to believe anything different.

So he asked her, "Torrie, is there anything you want to tell me? Anything we need to talk about?"

She looked him in the eyes and lied.

"No, baby. Why? Is something wrong?"

He let it go. Let her go.

That night, when she came home, everything unraveled.

She breezed through the door, stretching. "Ooooh, baby, I am exhausted. Did you eat? Want me to fix you something real quick?"

He sat in silence, watching her.

She turned, confused. "Amari, baby, what's wrong?"

He smiled. Something dark. Something dangerous.

"Where have you been, baby? I was worried about you."

She laughed lightly. "I told you, time slipped away. I was helping Sye with her contracts. Just trying to get her in the right place, you know?"

Look at her, lying through her teeth.

He played along, feigning interest in her work and asking follow-up questions. She had an answer for everything. Slick. Calculated.

So he set the trap.

"Oh, by the way," he said casually, "you left your phone today. A few texts came through. Whoever it was, they were lighting it up. Must be important."

He watched the slight twitch in her jaw as she walked over to grab her phone. The second she saw the messages, her face went pale.

She looked up at him. "Oh, you… already opened them?"

"Yeah," he said smoothly. "Like I said, they were coming back-to-back."

He saw the moment she knew she was caught.

The message was innocent enough:

Hey Torrie, you won't believe this. I'm in Atlanta for an interview with Minorities in Business. They called me yesterday and asked me to come out. Best part? I'm being featured in next month's issue. Just wanted to check in. Be good.

She had nothing to say. Nothing real, anyway. Just silence. Wide, guilty eyes.

"Torrie," he said, voice calm, eerily so, "is there something you want to tell me?"

She still told him no.

That night, they lay in bed—but they weren't alone.

Him. Her. The man who sent the flowers.

And Amari, the fool.

He hadn't yelled. Hadn't thrown anything. Hadn't done what some men would have done. He just wanted to talk.

Finally, she broke the silence.

"Amari?"

"Yeah, Torrie?"

She sighed, shifting to sit at the edge of the bed. "I owe you an apology."

He watched her. Waited.

She inhaled deeply. "There's no easy way to say this, so I'll just say it. I've been having an affair. The card and flowers at my office were from him. I wasn't with Sye. I was with him."

He heard her. But he couldn't process it.

An affair.

His wife had just told him she had been sleeping with another man.

His chest felt tight, his vision hazy. The rage came in waves, but beneath it was something worse. Betrayal.

And then, the dagger:

"Amari, I don't love him. I love you."

That was when he left. He grabbed his keys, walked out, and didn't stop until he was in a hotel room across town.

She didn't even try to stop him.

A clap of thunder outside jolted Amari back to the present.

Torrie had walked back into the kitchen, moving quietly as she loaded the dishwasher. She hadn't realized he was still watching her.

"Why are you staring at me, Amari?" Her voice was low. Unreadable.

"What?" He shook his head. *I wish you would just disappear.*

He stood and straightened his jacket. Before stepping through the door, he turned to her one last time.

"I didn't know this before," he said, his voice clear, firm. "But I know it now. I love you."

A pause.

"But I want a divorce."

And with that, he walked out, got into his car, and drove away.

For the first time since it all began, he felt free.

CHAPTER TEN

Symeria

It had been five days since Sye spoke to Torrie, and while that wasn't completely unusual, it still felt off. She figured there had to be a good reason—until she looked up on a Thursday afternoon and saw Taureen standing in her office doorway.

She was wearing jean shorts, a halter top, and sneakers.

That was when she knew something was wrong.

Sye blinked, trying to mask her surprise.

"Let me guess," she said, forcing a light tone. "Today is a Torrie-declared holiday. Is this the annual 'I Just Don't Feel Like It' holiday or the 'Give Me a Break Mental Health' holiday?"

Torrie attempted a smile but didn't quite make it.

"Sye," she exhaled, "I need to talk to you."

She immediately hit the intercom. "Darenda?"

"Yes, Miss Hayes?"

"Hold all my calls."

"Yes, Miss Hayes. Will do."

Sye stood, motioning for Torrie to sit on the couch. She sat beside her, taking in the dullness in her normally sharp eyes and the way her shoulders slumped like they were carrying too much weight.

"Torrie, baby, what's up?"

She took a breath, but her voice still cracked when she said, "Amari wants a divorce."

Damn.

Sye felt it like a physical blow, a tightness in her chest that wasn't even hers to bear.

"Noooo," she whispered, as if denying it could undo it.

Torrie started talking, unraveling the events of last Sunday, but before she could finish, the weight of it all crashed down on her—and she broke. Completely. Uncontrollable sobs wracked her body as she folded into herself.

Sye held her, pulling her close like a sister.

This pain, she knew.

Watching her break down sent Sye back to the moment her own heart shattered. It had been years since Lindsey, but heartbreak—real heartbreak—didn't just go away. It lingered. And seeing it happen to someone she loved? That hurt all over again.

 Trinity Sierra Sesay

"Why didn't you come to talk to me, Torrie? Why did you try to deal with this alone?" She handed her another tissue, watching as her fierce, vibrant friend sat in front of her, stripped of every ounce of her usual confidence.

"I... I didn't think he was serious. I thought he was just trying to be mean. Trying to hurt me." She blew her nose, then coughed.

Sye stood and grabbed a bottle of water from the fridge, pouring her a glass before handing it to her.

"Thank you," she murmured, sipping slowly as if it might help her swallow the truth. "Anyway, I need something from you, Sye. That's why I'm here."

"Okay," Sye said carefully. "What do you need?"

She set the glass down and met her eyes. "I was wondering if I could stay with you for about a month."

She didn't hesitate. "Of course."

"I know," Torrie nodded. "But I want you to understand why I'm asking."

"It doesn't matter why. The answer is still yes."

"No, Sye, listen to me." She exhaled deeply. "I'm not contesting the divorce. I'm giving him everything he wants. Everything. It doesn't matter to me anymore. I just... I don't want to be alone right now. I could get an apartment, I could buy another house, but I'm just not in that headspace. I need this transition to be as easy on my mind as possible."

Sye stared at her, amazed. Even at her lowest, Torrie was still thinking things through, still making sure she did what was best for her mental rather than just reacting. She admired that.

Sye moved closer and pulled her into another hug.

"It's going to be okay," she whispered. "We'll figure it out."

Just as the moment settled, a commotion erupted outside her office.

"Miss, you can't go in there," Darenda's high-pitched voice argued with someone.

Then the door flew open.

And there she was.

Dash.

"All right, break it up, break it up," she declared dramatically, flipping her locs over her shoulder. "I'm here now."

Torrie stiffened slightly, quickly wiping her tears. Dash, too busy side-eyeing Darenda, didn't notice.

"Miss Hayes," Darenda huffed, "I tried to stop her."

"It's okay, Darenda. This is my sister, Dash."

"Ooooh, thank God." Darenda sighed in relief. "Well, I'll leave you three alone then." She turned toward the door but hesitated. "Miss Hayes?"

"Yes, Darenda?"

"Am I still holding your calls?"

She checked the clock. "No, go ahead and put them through. Thank you."

Once Darenda left, Dash clapped her hands.

"What's up, chickas?"

Sye shook her head, smiling as she pulled her into a tight hug, then did the same to Torrie.

"How was the trip?" Sye asked.

"Long, but it's good to finally be home."

Torrie, pulling herself together, forced a small but genuine smile. "You look amazing."

She gave Dash a once-over: red capris, a sleek sleeveless knit top, and pristine Kenneth Cole flats.

"You're definitely serving a look today."

Dash smirked. "As always. Speaking of looks, Torrie… shouldn't you be at work?"

Torrie let out a half-laugh, half-scoff. "Sye likes to call it 'Miss Thang's Day'—when I just do what I feel like. No explanation needed."

Dash narrowed her eyes, sensing something deeper. "Mmm-hmm. And you, Miss Hayes, are hovering. Something's off here. What's up?"

Torrie nodded, silently giving her permission to tell her.

Sye sighed. "Torrie is getting a divorce."

Dash blinked, then adjusted.

"All right. Cool. So what's the plan for making his life miserable?"

Torrie and Sye burst into laughter. That was Dash—straight to business, no pity parties allowed.

Before they could respond, Darenda's voice came through the intercom.

"Miss Hayes, there's a Mr. Aaron Jensen on the line for you."

Both Dash and Torrie immediately side-eyed her.

Sye knew they'd picked up on the way she sat up straighter, the subtle inhale before answering.

"Thank you, Darenda. I'll take it."

She turned her chair, but she could hear them whispering.

"Did you see her reaction?" Dash asked.

"Mmm-hmm, she jumped for that call," Torrie added.

She groaned. "You girls do know I can hear you, right?"

Dash ignored her. "Sooo, is there something you want to tell us, Miss Mysterious?"

Torrie suddenly snapped her fingers. "Wait. Aaron? Aaron. That's JayInMotion, isn't it?"

 Trinity Sierra Sesay

Her grin was wicked.

Dash looked confused. "Who the hell is JayInMotion?"

Torrie smirked. "Sye met a man online. They've never met in person."

Dash turned to her, eyes wide. "Ohhhh, so you've got a Mr. Wonderful-dot-com situation?"

Sye sighed, rubbing her temple. "You girls are ridiculous."

Dash crossed her arms. "Well? When are you meeting him?"

Sye let out a breath, then smiled.

"Tonight. We're having dinner."

CHAPTER ELEVEN

Symeria

It was obvious to Symeria that if she was going to make it to dinner on time, she needed to leave her office now. It was already 5:30, and she was supposed to meet Aaron at six. The turn of events for the day had taken most of her time away. She tried to put up some of the folders on the desk and straightened up her office so that she could leave.

Darenda was already gone, so it was up to her to lock up. The only thing left for her to do was make sure that Dash was doing okay before she actually left. As she started dialing, she sat down in her chair, listening to the phone ring. It was strange how this morning she was living alone, and now, nine and a half hours later, she was running a bed and breakfast.

It was all good, though. She wouldn't have had it any other way.

She made a mental note to stop by Torrie's tomorrow. She knew she and Amari were going through a rough patch, but she never thought it would come to this. It just made her realize how fickle love could be.

Was it worth trying to find someone if nothing was guaranteed? It certainly didn't work out with Lindsey and her.

Every now and then, she found herself thinking about the day they first met. At the time, he was just the cute mixed guy who sat next to her during orientation. It didn't take long for them to become close friends, despite the fact that they were competing for a permanent spot in the company after graduation. It wasn't until after meeting him at the bookstore, close to the end of their internship, that she started to see him differently.

She was sitting at a table in the café when she saw him enter. He was casually dressed in jean shorts, a polo shirt, and sandals. She almost didn't recognize him since they had never seen each other outside of work before.

"Hey, you," she said.

She almost thought he didn't hear her as he took a few more steps, then stopped and turned around. Once he noticed it was her, he smiled and greeted her back. She stood up, and she was met with a deep embrace. It felt like he genuinely wanted to hug her. She was so caught up in the hug that she didn't even hear his question.

"Sye… what are you doing here?"

"Oh, sorry," she said, trying to regain her composure. "I'm just here checking out some new releases."

"Oh, so you're a reader?" he said, still flashing that beautiful smile.

"Yeah, I love to read. I don't have as much time as I would like to, but I still get it in when I can."

"So, are these the books that you're buying today?" he asked, flipping through the three books she had lying on the table.

"Actually, I think I'm only going to get these two. This one"—she pointed at one of the softcover romance novels—"doesn't seem to be that interesting."

"Enough about me. What about you?" she asked, trying to change the subject. "What are you doing here?"

"Oh, I just stopped in to pick up a couple of photography magazines."

"Photography?" she said, puzzled.

"Yes, photography. You sound surprised."

"I guess a little," she said, still looking confused. "You never mentioned that you were a photographer at work."

Lindsey smiled. "Yeah, that's true, but that's because I'm just private. I don't like people in my business at all. My personal life is mine, and I like to keep it that way."

She smiled and nodded. "Yeah, I understand. So, what kind of photography are you into?"

Lindsey gestured for her to walk with him as he moved toward the magazine section. "Well, I like anything nature-related, and now I'm starting to do weddings. Matter of fact, that's why I came in here. One of the photography magazines has a feature on shooting weddings, and I came to pick up a copy."

⸺ ❧ ⸺

That was the beginning of it. They walked around the bookstore for the next hour, just talking and looking at books and magazines. Then he suggested they get something to eat, so they did. Next thing you know, they were calling each other, texting each other, and sharing sly smiles and lingering eye contact at work.

They became almost inseparable, and neither of them could wait for the internship to end so they could be together freely—by day and by night. What got her the most was that they were genuinely friends first. They weren't trying to be a couple. Their friendship simply evolved. They didn't try to stop it; they just kept it quiet until the internship ended.

Neither of them was surprised when they both received offers to join the company full-time after graduation. But they were surprised when they both declined. Neither of them wanted to work for a cultureless company, and little did that company know—they both had options and plans.

A year later, they were officially a couple, and everyone around them knew it. They loved each other, and anyone who spent time around them could see it. She had been in relationships before, but she had never been in love. Lindsey was her first, and she welcomed it with open arms. She had also never been hurt by a man before. In fact, all her previous relationships ended amicably, with them remaining friends. But that all changed with him.

Who would've thought that the man she loved so much could hurt her the way he did?

It all started after the accident.

It was 8:30 when she got the call from Taylor, Lindsey's younger sister, telling her he had been in an accident. Her heart stopped. She couldn't tell what was happening—she just kept crying. Eventually, Sye found out he was at St. Joseph's Hospital.

I shouldn't have driven. I should have called an Uber or something. But in her mind, there was no time. Honestly, she didn't know how she got there in one piece. She was a wreck, and the lack of information made it worse.

After parking, she ran into the emergency room and found his family. They all looked worn down and distraught. She just knew the news had to be bad.

His mother saw her and reached out immediately. The moment they hugged, she began sobbing. Sye started crying, too—even though she had no clue what she was crying for. Before she could ask anything, his mother said he was in the ICU and had to be prepped for surgery.

"He's really bad," she said, barely able to speak. "He has a broken collarbone, collapsed lungs, and an injury to his spinal column, along with other abrasions. The doctor says he's going to live, but due to the spinal injury, walking..."

She couldn't finish. She broke down in sobs again.

Sye hugged her, then glanced around at everyone else, trying to force a hopeful smile. But it was hard.

Once the group began to sit, Taylor took her hand, and they found a seat together.

"How did this happen?" Sye asked.

"We were at my parents' house," Taylor began. "He and Sandy"—her older sister—"were in the garage. My dad mentioned the gutters were clogged with leaves, so they went out to clean them. Sandy said she thought the ladder was secure when Lynn went up, but a squirrel ran across his hand and startled him. He jumped, which made the ladder unstable.

"She said as the ladder started falling backward, Lynn jumped, but the way he landed... and then the ladder fell on him. He was unconscious. One of the neighbors, who's a physician, saw it happen and rushed over to help. By the time the ambulance arrived, Lynn was still out. It was just a freak accident."

She squeezed Sye's hand. "I'm glad we were all there."

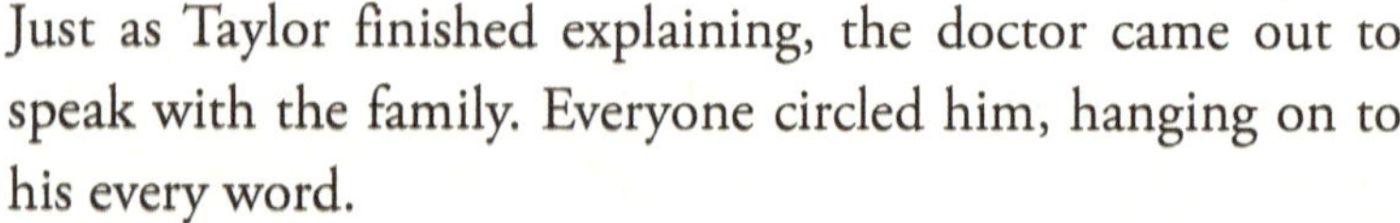

Just as Taylor finished explaining, the doctor came out to speak with the family. Everyone circled him, hanging on to his every word.

"The surgery went well," he said. "There's a lot of swelling around the spine, so we won't know about potential paralysis until the swelling goes down."

He allowed only the parents to visit. Sye remained in the lobby with Taylor until she was ready to leave.

The next day, Taylor called Sye and told her not to come to the hospital—he still couldn't have visitors other than his parents since he remained in the ICU. Sye understood, but the wait was agonizing.

On the third day came the good news: he was awake and being moved out of the ICU. Visitors were now allowed. They still didn't know about the paralysis, but his prognosis was improving.

When Symeria arrived at the hospital, she was greeted by his mother, who pulled her into a warm embrace, wearing her usual radiant smile.

Sye remembered thinking, *She really does like me.* And she smiled to herself.

"You're smiling today, Mother. You look happy. What's the word?"

"Oh, Sye," she said, nearly bursting, "The doctor said there's no paralysis. Just broken bones and a lot of soreness. He's going to need rehab, but he's going to be okay."

Sye exhaled with relief. "Can I see him?"

"Sure, baby, go on in. We're going to get something to eat—we'll be right back. Can we bring you anything?"

"No, I'm good. Thanks for asking, though."

Sye stepped into the room. The first thing she noticed were the bandages: his head, chest, arm, and leg, which had been propped up. She tried not to show her concern, but he saw it anyway.

"Hey, you," she said softly.

"Hey to you, too," he replied, coughing as he spoke.

She moved closer. She wanted to hug him, but didn't want to cause him pain. Instead, she placed her hand on his and gazed into his eyes.

"You know," she said, half smiling, "if you really wanted a break from me, you didn't have to go through all this. You could've just asked."

Her smile grew, teasing. He struggled a little but managed a chuckle.

"Is that right?" he said, smiling. Their eyes stayed locked.

"I love you," he whispered.

He had said it before, but this time... this time, it meant more.

Lindsey spent two weeks in the hospital. Upon his release, he moved in with Sye—not out of a declaration of love, but because it made sense. His apartment had stairs. So did his parents' and sisters' homes. Sye's place was one level with an open floor plan. It was the most logical place to recover.

And she wanted to help. *That's what someone in love does, right?*

The doctor said it would be at least six to eight months before he'd be fully recovered and cleared to drive. In two months of successful rehab, he'd be able to work from home.

Sye surprised herself when she offered for him to move in. She had always been against living with a man she was dating—not for religious reasons, just on principle. *If a man already has everything, what's left to work toward in the relationship?*

As the old adage goes, *Why buy the cow when you can get the milk for free?*

But this was different. She was helping the man she loved recover in comfort. And for her, that was a no-brainer.

⚬⚬⚬

After four months of rehab, the recovery was going well. Lindsey was getting stronger, slowly starting to walk on his own with assistance—if only for a few moments. One of the challenges they were facing, however, was cohabitation etiquette. Both of them were used to living alone, so little things like the television volume, lights on versus lights off, and the room temperature all became contentious. She understood that he was very independent and despised not being able to go about as he would have liked, but she was sacrificing too—and she needed him to know it.

At six months and four days, he was cleared to move back into his townhouse and return to work full-time. He was cleared to drive and live his life the way he wanted—and boy, did he. That's when the issues began.

Once he was fully moved back into his place, she expected an adjustment period. After all, she had spent six months waiting on him hand and foot. So when he didn't call her, or they didn't speak for a few days, she wasn't immediately concerned. But by the second week, when he still wasn't answering her calls, she was pissed.

The first issue came when she went to check on him. She had called on her way over, but it went straight to voicemail. When she arrived, his car was in the driveway, so she knew he was home. Instead of ringing the bell, she used her key—and there he was, sitting on the couch, eating wings and drinking a beer, watching television.

"I called you," she said, obviously agitated.

"Yeah, I saw that," he replied casually. "I couldn't get to the phone before you hung up."

"Did you think of calling back?"

He looked at her, clearly annoyed, and took a swig of his beer. "I was going to call you later, Sye."

"Oh really?" There was no hiding her emotions.

"What is the problem, Sye? I said I was going to call you. Damn."

"Lindsey, why are you acting like I'm the one at fault here? I haven't heard from you since you moved back, and now you're ignoring my calls?"

He took a breath. "Look, I just need some space. I need to get back into my life as it was before the accident, that's all. Can you do that? Can you give me some space?"

She wasn't quite sure what this *space* thing really meant— but it eventually became clear.

The second incident came on a Saturday morning around 7:30. He called her, out of nowhere, to say that he wanted the key to his house back. Since he was fully recovered, he saw no reason for her to have it anymore. She reminded him that he still had a key to her place.

"Yeah, I know. I'm planning to give it back to you, too," he said.

She asked him what this all meant. He didn't answer.

"Just trying to get back to a semblance of normalcy. Prior to the accident, we didn't have each other's keys," he said.

She didn't press it. She offered to drop the key off, but he insisted they meet somewhere for the trade-off. Her intuition told her this wasn't just about returning keys. Something deeper was happening.

After another week of lackluster conversation and forced pleasantries, he said they needed to meet and talk. He felt they should clear the air. She agreed.

They met at a restaurant they used to frequent when things between them were good. He ordered their usual drinks and food, and then he started talking.

He admitted things felt awkward between them and that he blamed himself for the growing distance. He said the accident had changed him—that coming so close to death had shifted his priorities. His second chance at life wasn't something he was taking lightly.

He thanked her. Sincerely. He acknowledged the ways she cared for him, opened her home to him, changed her routine for him. He knew she had loved him through it all.

But then came the shift.

"Even with all of that," he said, "it's still not enough."

He explained that things were different now. They weren't the same, because one of them—at least one of them—was not the same.

She was confused. She knew he had been through a life-altering experience, but what exactly was he saying?

Agitated, she blurted out, "Are you seeing someone else?"

Startled, he said, "What? No! No. I'm not seeing someone else."

"Then what, Lindsey? What are you talking about?"

He took a sip of water, then carefully placed the glass down on the cocktail napkin beside his silverware.

"What I'm trying to say to you, Sye, is that I love you. I really do. But I can no longer be in a relationship with you."

"What?" She felt as if her heart had dropped out of her chest. *Did this man, whom I nursed back to health and gave my life to for over six months, just say he loves me—but can't be with me?*

"I don't understand," she said, feeling deflated. "You just said you love me."

"I do, Sye. Really, I do. But we're no longer compatible."

"Compatible?" she echoed.

"Yes, compatible. What you don't know is—I've converted to Islam. I'm a Muslim now. And I know that you're very spiritual, but you've never expressed interest in being Muslim. I need to be with someone who shares my religious values. Otherwise, the relationship won't work."

Believe me, this was a very hard decision for me to make. I promised Allah that if He healed me—"

"What?" she interrupted. "What? You promised Him what? That He could have you if He healed you? Is that it?"

"Yes, pretty much. Sye, I'm sorry. I didn't mean for anything like this to happen. I have been trying to figure out a way to tell you without hurting you."

"Hurting me?" she said, pointing toward herself. "When did all of this happen? I mean, Muslim? Who do you know that is a Muslim? You know what, Lynn, never mind. I really don't want to know. I don't care." She got up from the table.

"Sye, wait!" he said, gently pulling her back down to her seat. "Let me explain. At the hospital, one of the chaplains—a Muslim—came to my room. He was looking for someone else and had the wrong room number. He noticed I had the Lakers game on and was a fan. We started talking—just basketball stuff at first—and then other things. Not religion. He never brought it up. One day, I asked him about Islam because I was curious, and he talked to me about it. The next day, he brought me literature and I started reading."

"Remember when you asked me, once I was cleared to drive, where I was going? You joked about it being to play golf, but in actuality, my first trip was to the mosque. I felt something there that I hadn't felt before. I know you didn't notice, but during those six months while you were working, I was at home reading the Quran and doing research. I wanted to be sure. And when I got to the mosque after prayer, I was."

"How did I not know any of this?"

"I kept it hidden because I wasn't certain. When I finally was, I didn't know how to tell you. Honestly, I think it would've been easier to tell you I was cheating than this."

She held back tears. It felt like betrayal. "You said you were sorry? What exactly are you sorry for, Lindsey?"

"I'm sorry that I broke your heart. And that I can't choose you."

Just like that, he and she were no more.

He was right. Now that she thought about it, it would have been easier if he had just cheated. At least that, she could have understood. But to know he made a conscious choice—and that choice wasn't her? That was worse.

It was the last time she ever truly loved a man. No one since had come close.

The sound of Dash's voice on the phone pulled her back to the present.

Sye told her the time and location of the date for safety, then hung up. As she moved through the office, turning off lights and locking doors, it hit her: she was going on a date with a complete stranger. She could still cancel. But she didn't. She shook off the nerves, got in the car, and drove.

⸺◦◦◦⸺

It should have only taken about ten minutes to get to Broad Street from Television Circle. But with rush-hour traffic, it was closer to twenty. Still, Sye was determined to have a decent time. Free dinner, good drinks, and no need to see him again after—it could be worse.

After parking, she checked her hair, lipstick, and nose in the mirror. "Perfect," she mouthed before stepping out of the car.

"Good evening, Madame. How many in your party?" the host asked as she entered.

"Actually, I'm meeting someone here. Aaron Jensen."

"Of course. Right this way."

The tall, olive-skinned host with striking green eyes led her toward the back. A tall, chocolate-skinned man in beige slacks stood as they approached. Neatly trimmed goatee, diamond stud in his left ear, short-cropped curly hair. He wasn't Idris, but he was decent.

"Symeria, how are you? I'm Aaron."

"Hello, Aaron," she said with a polite smile. "Nice to meet you."

He extended his hand, then pulled out her chair like a gentleman. She could feel his eyes appreciating her dress.

"Nice outfit," he said.

"Thanks," she replied, smiling. "You look handsome yourself."

Though she couldn't help but notice the black shoes clashing with all that beige.

"So," Aaron said, settling in, "you're the one who's been keeping me up at night."

She arched an eyebrow. "Me? No, I think you've got the wrong person."

The waiter arrived with a bottle of Chardonnay.

"Would you like to sample?" he asked.

"No," she answered. "I'd prefer a glass of sparkling Demi-Sec."

"I'll have a Dark and Stormy," Aaron added.

The waiter nodded, took their drink orders, and left them with two menus.

"I'm really glad we finally got to meet in person," Aaron said, flashing a boyish grin. "You're beautiful."

"Thank you," she said, flipping open the menu. "So, what's good here?"

"It's my first time here," he admitted. "I heard it's good, so we'll see."

She ordered the *Eminolaille sauce Roquefort*—thinly sliced fillet of chicken with Roquefort sauce and sautéed potatoes. Aaron chose the *Terrine de Saumon aux Épinards*—salmon and spinach terrine with special rice.

The waiter returned with French bread, a cheese tray with six varieties, and two salads.

"So," Aaron said as he spread cheese on his bread, "tell me again—why is someone as beautiful as you still single?"

The question caught her off guard. "I tell you what, Aaron. Why don't you tell me your story first? Then maybe I'll tell you mine."

"Okay, are you being shy now or just difficult?" he smirked. "I don't want to confuse the two. Besides, I believe in ladies first—and you are one hell of a lady."

She chuckled. "Well, thank you for noticing. But I really would like to hear about you."

Aaron exhaled. "Alright, but I should warn you: my story isn't uncommon. Pretty regular, in fact." He took a sip of water. "Do you know the number one reason for the high divorce rate?"

She rolled her eyes. "Infidelity."

"Exactly," he said. "And that's my story in a nutshell."

She sipped her wine, narrowing her eyes. "Go ahead, Aaron. Spit it out. What are you saying?"

He leaned forward. "I know what you're thinking. 'Why do men cheat? What is it that women do to drive men to stray?' But that's where most women get it wrong."

"Wrong?" she said, setting down her glass. "What's there to be wrong about? You just admitted you cheated. There had to be a reason, right?"

"No, actually, there wasn't."

"There wasn't?"

He shook his head. "Nope. You have to understand men. Unlike women, who might cheat because of emotional neglect, frustration, or lack of attention, men don't always need a reason. A man doesn't have to be unhappy to desire another woman."

She stared. "Go on."

"I was in love with my wife. There were no major problems. We had the usual ups and downs, but nothing serious. Our sex life was healthy. Our connection was strong. I knew, without a doubt, that she loved me. She showed it every day."

"So why cheat?" she asked, genuinely confused.

Aaron sighed. "One day, I met someone I was physically attracted to. And I went for her. No emotional connection. No deep longing. Just opportunity. And eventually, my wife found out. After the third time, she was done."

She folded her arms. "So let me get this straight: you had a great marriage and a loyal wife, and you still stepped out?"

Aaron nodded. "Yeah."

"Sooo... what does that make you now? A reformed player? A man still figuring it out?"

"It makes me human. It makes me someone who made mistakes," he said evenly. "But my lifestyle isn't like that anymore. I don't have time or energy for games."

She studied him. "So now what? Are you looking for something serious, or are you just seeing what's out there?"

"I want something real," he said simply. "No games."

She nodded slowly. "We'll see."

Aaron leaned in. "Alright, your turn. What's your story?"

She took a deep breath and locked eyes with him. "I'm a lesbian."

Aaron choked on his drink, then burst into laughter. "Okay, okay, you got me."

The waiter returned with their salads.

Aaron reached for her hand. "Mind if I bless the food?"

She hesitated but let him. His hands were warm. A little too familiar, but she let it slide.

As they started eating, Aaron smirked. "Now, back to your story, Miss Symeria."

She sighed. "Fine. Here's the express version: I don't know why I'm single. I know why my last relationship ended. But as for why I'm single now? No clue."

Aaron listened intently. "Go on."

"The last relationship I was in... I constantly felt like I was in it alone. The body was there. The voice was there. But the commitment wasn't. I kept trying, but eventually, it faded."

Aaron smiled knowingly. "Well, I can tell you this—you won't have that problem with me."

She forced a smile while nudging the last tomato on her plate. "We'll see."

CHAPTER TWELVE

Taureen

Torrie didn't care how many times she went over it in her head; she still couldn't believe she was actually moving out of her house. The house she and Amari had built together.

It felt unreal.

On one hand, she kept telling herself this wasn't really happening. Any minute now, Amari would walk through the door, take her by the hand, and say, *Torrie, baby, let's talk about this. Let's work this out.* But on the other hand, she was here, loading boxes into her car, preparing to move into her new, temporary residence: Hotel Symeria of Savannah.

Torrie never meant to hurt Amari.

Leaning against her car, she found herself lost in the memory of how it all started, how she first laid eyes on Jarrod.

He had walked into the courtroom late that day, supposed to present probation records for a client of hers, some black male caught up in a divorce while facing armed robbery charges.

When Jarrod entered, he commanded the attention of the entire room.

At 5'10, he had a strong, self-assured presence, with smooth, chocolate skin and short, salt-and-pepper hair that only added to his distinguished appearance. No facial hair, no piercings, just clean, crisp lines and an air of refinement. But it was his *eyes* that captivated her, almond-shaped, framed by stylish Versace glasses, and *too* knowing.

Torrie had always been a sucker for a man who looked *smart.*

It had started as a simple conversation about a case. But somehow, the conversation just kept going.

And then there was coffee.

And then more coffee.

And before she knew it, there was something *else* between them.

At first, she couldn't figure out what exactly drew her to him. Was it his attention? The way he made her feel seen? Or was it something deeper, something missing from her marriage?

She had tried to push the thoughts aside. Had tried to fix things at home.

That week, she had made love to Amari four times. And yet, each time, she was left lying awake, unsatisfied, staring at the ceiling while he drifted off, *completely* unaware.

She wanted *more*.

And then trouble showed up, wearing a perfectly tailored turquoise Perry Ellis suit.

Jarrod stopped by her office unexpectedly one afternoon, leaning against the doorframe like he belonged there.

"Dinner tonight?" he asked, as casually as if he were asking about the weather.

Torrie hesitated, "Dinner?"

"Just dinner. Nothing more."

It wasn't supposed to be anything. Amari was stuck in Jacksonville for yet another engineering conference. And *dinner* was harmless. Just a meal. Just conversation.

Right?

Except, when she arrived, she realized dinner wouldn't be at a restaurant.

Jarrod had cooked.

She should have walked away then. Should have made an excuse and left. But she didn't.

She sat at his kitchen island while he poured her a glass of water, watching as he moved effortlessly through his home: impeccably decorated, warm, inviting. He told her about his sisters and his daughter and how they had helped him with the décor. His voice was smooth, the conversation easy.

And then the rain started.

The downpour was so heavy that it rattled the windows. Flash flood warnings lit up her phone. She knew Savannah well enough to understand that driving in this weather would be reckless.

"You can't drive in this," Jarrod said simply, "Stay a while."

She had nodded, more to herself than to him.

And then there was the kiss.

She hadn't planned it. Hadn't anticipated the way it would feel, *like air after drowning.*

Jarrod kissed her like he *knew* her, like he had studied her, like he understood the things she had never spoken aloud. His lips trailed her neck, his breath warm against her skin, and before she could think, before she could *stop*, he was leading her toward his bedroom.

"Relax," he had whispered against her ear, "I won't hurt you."

But he *had*. Not in the way he meant, but in a way far worse.

Because after that night, she knew there was no going back.

⸺⸺❈⸺⸺

Torrie shook herself from the memory, inhaling deeply as she loaded the last box into her trunk.

She had ended things with Jarrod because the guilt was too much. Because she loved Amari. Because what she had shared with Jarrod, she *wanted* to share with her husband.

But it was too late.

Now, she was here, standing in her driveway, preparing to leave the life she had built.

And Amari?

He wasn't stopping her.

CHAPTER THIRTEEN

Dash

Dash knew that moving back to Savannah would be bitter-sweet. She loved this city, she really did, but it was boring as hell. From what she had heard, it was progressing somewhat, but at a snail's pace.

Dash had never been one to go backward, and her return to this city felt exactly like that. She needed to figure out how to make her life here more comfortable, especially if she planned on staying for a while.

The chime of the doorbell startled Dash. She frowned, wondering why Sye even had one installed in the first place.

"Now, who the hell is that?" she muttered, walking toward the door.

On the other side stood a tall, brown-skinned man.

"Yes, can I help you?"

"It's me, Amari."

Dash opened the door and gave him a quick once-over. "Sye's not in. I'm her sister, Dash."

"Oh, my bad, I thought you were…"

"Well, I'm not. What do you want?"

"Um, I just wanted to talk to her about something."

"Sounds serious. Can I help?"

Amari smirked. "You don't even know who I am, but you're offering me your ear? That's special."

"I know who you are, Amari. I said I was Symeria's sister, not her girlfriend. You're Torrie's husband, aren't you?"

"Yes."

"Come on in. Sye should be home shortly. You're welcome to wait if you would like."

"I knew Sye had a sister, but I didn't know she was so beautiful. Aren't you in the military or something?"

"Was," she corrected. "I just retired."

"Oh, sounds interesting. What exactly did you do?"

Dash held back a sigh. She wasn't in the mood for small talk. "I was a medic. I healed people for a living." She stepped aside, allowing him to enter. "So, what's ailing you, Mr. Amari? Something I can help with? I'm a r-e-a-l good listener." Dash dragged out the words, watching his reaction.

"I don't usually do this, but since I'm here, I might as well talk."

Dash smiled. *That's what they all say.* "Cool. Talk to me."

Amari hesitated before the words slowly came out. "Torrie and I are getting a divorce. She cheated on me, and I want to know from Symeria if she knew. And if she did, why didn't she tell me?"

Dash raised an eyebrow. "Interesting."

"What?"

"Your inability to identify your real problem."

Amari's nose flared slightly. "What does that mean?"

"Well, you're saying you came here to find out if Sye knew about Torrie's infidelity. I can tell you she didn't, but even if she did, do you really want to hear it from her? Or do you want to hear it from your wife?" Dash softened her voice, trying to ease the tension building in him. "Your real problem is that you haven't had time to vent."

Dash moved closer, lightly fingering his hair, locking eyes with him. The touch seemed to soothe his anger, replacing it with something more curious.

"Are you always this forward?" Amari asked, trying to move away, but he was caught in the intensity of her gaze.

"You have no idea."

Dash wasn't surprised when Amari tried to deny her advances. They always did. But by the time she knew it, Amari was butt naked and on his back in her bed.

She had tried to be nice, let him be the dominant one, but that didn't work; he was awful in bed. Dash didn't even get a rise. That's when she gave up on being accommodating and took control. *Look at him,* she thought, *sweating profusely like he did something.* Men like him thought sex was all about pumping their manhood in and out as if that alone did the job.

Dash pulled out her handcuffs from the nightstand and clipped them on in one smooth motion. Then she covered his mouth with a scarf. To secure his ankles, she took the two leather straps she had and tied them to the bed frame. *I will never get rid of this bed,* she thought. *She loved it; poles and all.*

Amari squirmed, looking up at her wide-eyed as if she intended to murder him. He kept asking stupid questions.

"You're not going to hurt me, are you?"

"You are gonna let me out of this, right?"

Dash just smiled. *He has no idea.*

Dash studied Amari, the flicker of anticipation in his eyes. She smirked, enjoying the tension between them.

Slowly, she leaned in, letting her lips graze just close enough to send a shiver through him. She teased him, drawing out the moment with calculated precision, just enough to make him desperate for more.

Her fingers danced over his skin, tracing slow, deliberate patterns while her lips followed. A quiet groan escaped him, his breathing uneven as she continued.

For several minutes, the game remained in her control: push, pull, let go. His restraint unraveled under her touch, his body responding exactly as she intended.

Then, just as the moment escalated, she pulled away.

Silence stretched between them. He blinked up at her, chest rising and falling with ragged breaths as realization set in.

Dash smirked. *Men are weak.*

Minutes later, Amari was already out cold, his body slack with exhaustion from the buildup alone.

Shaking her head, Dash nudged him, but he barely stirred. She rolled her eyes, slipping off the bed and grabbing her robe.

"Did I really just knock him out?"

She chuckled to herself, amused. "Another one down."

After untying him, she let him sleep. He was going to be one sore brother in the morning. Dash slipped on her calf-length bathrobe, embroidered with the letter *D* on the upper left shoulder, and mused at how easy men were no matter how strong they thought they were.

She had just finished brushing her teeth when she heard the groggy sounds of Amari waking up. As she was about to exit the room, she glanced back at him, still spread out across her king-sized pillow-top mattress.

"Where are you going?" he asked.

Dash folded her arms. "I'm going to the kitchen, and I suggest you get up, get dressed, and leave before anyone sees you."

"Right, right, good thinking."

She sauntered downstairs into the kitchen. Just as she pulled the leftover pizza out of the refrigerator, Sye walked in. Dash glanced at her sister, unfazed by her presence despite Amari still being in her bed.

"What's up, girl? How ya livin'?"

Sye eyed her sister suspiciously. "Sounds like someone had a good night."

Dash smirked. "What makes you say that?"

Before Sye could answer, a voice called out.

"Goodnight, Dash."

Amari darted out of the house like a sprinter at the Kentucky Derby.

Sye stared at Dash in disbelief. "Was that Amari?"

"Yep."

"Okay… why was he here? And why did he leave in such a hurry?"

Dash popped a bite of pizza into her mouth. "He came to see you. Wanted to talk about whether you knew about Torrie's affair, blah, blah, I don't know. But you weren't here."

"Why would he want to talk to me about it?"

"Shouldn't you be asking him that?"

Sye narrowed her eyes. "If he wanted to talk, why did he leave?"

Dash leaned against the counter, chewing thoughtfully. "One thing led to another."

Sye's face darkened. "Dash… please tell me you didn't sleep with him."

Dash took another bite. "Relax, Sye. We didn't have sex."

Sye let out a breath of relief.

"We just cuddled," Dash added, smirking.

Sye groaned. "I'm going to bed."

CHAPTER FOURTEEN

Symeria

It was clear after the date with Aaron, he was not Sye's cup of tea. She couldn't see herself trusting him if they were ever to be serious about one another. In the back of her mind, she would always be wondering if he was truly being faithful to her. It also didn't help that he still lived with his wife. He had the audacity to call her his "roommate." What kind of ignorance was that? The worst part is that he actually believed that she should be more understanding. Sye still can't believe he had the nerve to say, "For someone with so much going for her, you sure are closed-minded about life." Yeah, she's closed-minded to being played for a fool.

What was it about men when they didn't get their way? They like to attack a girl's education, accomplishments, and character. What was that about?

Take, for instance, Greg, the second guy she met online, aka *ChocolateLover69*. Normally, she wouldn't have given him the time of day because of his name.

"I mean, really, could you be more full of yourself?"

But just for fun, she responded to his DM.

ChocolateLover69: Hello Love, I see you are in Savannah. Hi, my name is Chocolate, and yours?

Real original. Sye typed out: EveAfterDark

ChocolateLover69: No baby, what is your REAL name?

The nerve. She spelled it out again, just to be petty: E-V-E

ChocolateLover69: lol. Ok, I see. You are a little leery, but that's fine. By the end of this convo, I'll have the name.

She doubted that. He went through the usual questions: age, sex, race. She kept it brief: Black female. He seemed to accept that she wasn't giving him much, and soon, the conversation became easier.

They messaged back and forth for about an hour. Surprisingly, it was decent, especially since she had nothing else to do. He liked the usual: movies, sports, eating out, romantic walks, poetry. All the things women love to hear.

She was waiting for the inevitable *so do you have a pic?* question, but after an hour, it never came. So, she asked him instead.

EveAfterDark: Do you have a photo to share?

ChocolateLover69: NOPE!

EveAfterDark: Dang, why say it like that?

ChocolateLover69: Because I don't want you to be swayed by my handsomeness in a photo and decide you want to meet me. I want you to get to know me first.

She smirked. *Oh, so we were playing mystery man now? Fine.*

They talked for about a week, and while she was chatting with others, he held most of her attention. Against her better judgment, she actually started looking forward to his messages.

One night, he surprised her.

ChocolateLover69: Silo?

EveAfterDark: Yes, Chocolate?

ChocolateLover69: I'd like to meet you in person.

She hesitated for a second before responding.

EveAfterDark: Really? When?

ChocolateLover69: You tell me. You're the one with a busy schedule.

EveAfterDark: Hmmm. Well, is this going to be a date? Or just a meeting?

ChocolateLover69: How about a meeting? Over coffee?

EveAfterDark: How about Barnes & Noble on Abercorn, across from the mall?

ChocolateLover69: Cool. When?

EveAfterDark: This evening after work.

She held her breath.

ChocolateLover69: Yes, that works for me.

Boy, was I happy to hear that.

ChocolateLover69: How will I know you?

EveAfterDark: I'll be the one wearing apple green and beige.

ChocolateLover69: Apple green?

EveAfterDark: Yes, like the color of a green apple.

ChocolateLover69: Oh, ok. I think I know. How about 5:30?

EveAfterDark: That'll be fine. See you then.

Excitement turned into dread when she actually saw him in person. At first, she thought, *Nope, can't be him,* but when he locked eyes with her, she knew she was in trouble.

This man was all of 5'5 and maybe 320 pounds. His complexion was deep blue-black, which wouldn't have been an issue, but the nappy half-afro with a missing front tooth? The long fingernails that put hers to shame? And to top it all off, he was standing there in a purple suit.

I mean, really? Purple? Oh, hell no.

"EveAfterDark?" he asked.

She wanted to say *No, wrong person,* but the yes slipped out before she could stop it.

"Hi, I'm ChocolateLover69. My name is Greg, and you are?"

Dumbass. You just told me your name. "Me? Uh, my name is... Sye."

"You are beautiful, Sye. What a pretty name. What does it stand for?"

"It just stands for Sye." She was scrambling for an escape plan.

"Would you like some coffee?"

"No, no. I'm not staying long, and it's too late for coffee; it'll keep me up all night."

He grinned. "So maybe we can just sit and talk?"

She sighed. "Fine."

Greg spent the next thirty minutes talking about how wonderful he was. He went on and on about his ideal woman, kitchen skills, and passion for romance. When Sye closed her eyes, he sounded decent. But opening them again? An eyesore.

She figured she'd appease him since she'd never see him again anyway.

"So, Greg," she interrupted his self-love fest, "how'd you come up with your screen name?"

He smirked. "That's not obvious?"

"Nope."

"Well, I'm a true lover of chocolate."

She blinked. "Chocolate?"

"Yes! The sweet brown cocoa goodness. Chocolate-covered raisins, almonds, cake, cookies. Oooh, I just love it."

This fool moaned. *Moaned.*

That was her cue.

"Greg! Greg!" She snapped her fingers.

"Oh, sorry! I get excited talking about chocolate."

"Uh-huh. So... what's the 69 for?"

He winked. "My birthday is in July. I'm a Cancer. The 69 represents my zodiac sign."

"Right..." I shot up. "Well, I gotta go."

"So soon?"

"Yes, early day tomorrow."

"Ok, so when can we see each other again?"

"Let's talk about it tonight when we're online, okay?"

"Sure," he beamed.

She practically ran to her car.

By the time she got home, she blocked him. But before she did, she noticed a final message:

ChocolateLover69: *Sye, I was very disappointed in our meeting. You were misleading. Through you, I learned people aren't always what they seem. For an educated woman, you're actually kind of blonde. I don't think you're very smart.*

She read it twice. Then shrugged.

Go figure.

CHAPTER FIFTEEN

Dash

Dash didn't know what it was about pancakes, but she loved them, and IHOP was her spot. There was something about the fluffy stacks drenched in syrup that just made life better. She always enjoyed getting up early on the weekends and treating herself to breakfast. She and Robert used to meet here, grabbing a newspaper, sipping coffee, sitting for hours just talking and enjoying each other's company.

The only difference now? She was here alone.

And for once, she was okay with that.

Just as she settled in, fork in hand, her phone vibrated against the table. She glanced at the screen and let out a groan. Damn, so much for peace and quiet.

"Dash," the deep baritone called out before she could even say hello.

She rolled her eyes. *Him.* She knew that voice anywhere.

"Damn, just as I was starting to enjoy my morning, you call," she said, not bothering to mask her irritation.

"Dash, dear," the voice drawled. "So, finally, we speak again."

She sighed, placing her fork down and leaning back in the booth. He still had that voice. The kind that could make a woman weak if she let it. Fortunately, she wasn't that woman. Not anymore.

"Look, I'm not even going to ask how you got my number because I know you're resourceful," she said, skipping the formalities, "So, I'll get straight to the point. What do you want?"

"Want?" he repeated, amused. "Oh, Dash, you think I'm calling because I want something from you? No, that would be too easy. I don't want anything…" He let the words hang for a beat. "What I want is you."

If she laughed any harder, she would've blown a vein in her forehead.

"Did you just say you want me?" she asked, wiping the tears from her eyes. "Man, be for real."

"Are you laughing?" he asked, his voice tightening. "Why does it sound like you're laughing?"

"Because I am laughing," Dash said, still amused. "You can't be serious."

But the next words that came through the line wiped the smirk off her face.

 Trinity Sierra Sesay

"I'm laughing too," he said, his tone darker now. "Laughing because after everything you've done, after the chaos you created in my life, you actually have the audacity to think you have options. You don't, Dash. You never did."

She stiffened.

"I know exactly what you did," he continued. "And I intend to make you pay for it. I don't know how long it'll take. I don't know how I'll do it. But just know this: until I'm satisfied, you'll be looking over your shoulder. Every. Single. Day."

And just like that, the call went dead.

Dash stared at her phone, still pressed to her ear, the silence humming in her chest.

A threat.

Not just a threat; a promise.

She exhaled, tossed her phone onto the table, and picked up her fork again.

The thing was, she didn't know if she was more amused that he was still pissed, or more irritated that he actually thought she cared.

He got exactly what he deserved.

And if he wanted war, he picked the wrong damn woman.

Smirking, she cut into her pancakes and took a bite.

Let him watch his back, too.

CHAPTER SIXTEEN

Amari

Six months.

The judge said they had to wait six whole months before the divorce could be finalized.

Six months of being legally tied to a woman he wanted nothing to do with.

Six months of forced couples therapy.

Six months of sitting across from her, listening to excuses, when he already knew the truth.

And to top it all off? A weekend couples retreat.

A damn retreat!

Why the hell would he want to spend an entire weekend "rekindling" something he was actively trying to end?

Amari clenched his fists so hard that his knuckles cracked. He was so angry that he could barely see straight.

But the part that got him the most?

Torrie's performance in the judge's chambers.

Oh, she played her role perfectly, all soft-spoken, trembling hands and tear-filled eyes. The whole courtroom was watching her unravel like some heartbroken victim.

At first, the judge, a man, thank God, wasn't buying it. He told her to pull herself together and get to the point.

But then?

She dropped the damn bomb.

"Your Honor," she sniffled, "I am guilty of everything my husband has accused me of. I had an affair, I lied, and if that warrants a divorce, then so be it.

But even a criminal gets a chance to plead their case.

And I am not a criminal.

I have yet to be able to tell my side of the story.

My husband won't talk to me. He won't listen. He won't even look at me.

How can a marriage, one sanctioned by our families, our friends, and God, be dissolved without even a chance for real discussion?

The same way it took time to build this marriage—dating, pre-marital counseling, wedding preparations, and vows—I believe divorce should be given that same time.

 Trinity Sierra Sesay

I love my husband. If this is what he wants, I won't fight him. But I do believe he owes me, at the very least, an opportunity to speak. And he should, at the very least, be willing to listen."

Even he almost fell for that bullshit.

Almost.

If Amari never thought Torrie was a damn good lawyer before, she sure as hell proved it now.

Because before he knew it, the judge was nodding his head, stroking his beard, and asking, "Mrs. Hayes, what activities do you believe would best facilitate this process?"

And what did Torrie say?

Couples therapy. A six-month waiting period. And a couples retreat.

Damn lawyers.

Amari leaned back in his chair, rubbing his temples.

If Torrie thought this little delay was going to change anything, she was deluding herself.

His mind was made up.

He was out.

CHAPTER SEVENTEEN

Taureen

Torrie's phone wouldn't stop ringing as she pulled into the driveway of her temporary home.

She gripped the steering wheel, exhaling before finally answering on the second ring.

"Hello, this is Taureen."

"Torrie, it's Sye."

Torrie could hear the concern laced in her best friend's voice. She already knew what was coming.

"How did it go in court? I was going to wait until later, but I figured I'd call now just to check on you. So, how did it go?"

Torrie shut off the ignition, rubbing her temple with her free hand.

"Well enough. I know Amari is mad as hell right now, but he left me no other choice."

"No other choice?" Sye repeated.

Torrie huffed, "He just up and decided that he wanted a divorce, Sye. Just like that! Over what? A lapse in judgment? A small mistake?"

The bitterness in her own voice startled her.

She clenched her jaw. "And the fact that he can't see that he played a part in this is unreal. I mean, really, Sye, if he had just paid me a little more attention, none of this would have happened."

Silence.

Then, finally, "Torrie…"

That one word, the way Sye said it so carefully, made her stomach tighten.

"You said he left you no other choice. What did you do?"

Torrie rolled her eyes, leaning her head against the headrest.

"Nothing that any other woman wouldn't have done."

Sye's voice sharpened, "Please tell me you didn't play the 'I'm pregnant' game."

Torrie burst into laughter.

"No, no, nothing like that. I just…" she smirked, rubbing her forehead, "Let's just say I had a moment in the judge's chambers. I broke down. Pleaded my case."

 Trinity Sierra Sesay

The restrained laughter on the other end of the phone made Torrie groan.

She covered her face, the scene replaying in her mind. *Damn, I really did put on a show, huh?*

But it had to be done.

"Look," she sighed, "all I want is for Amari to talk to me. Really talk to me. Listen to me. I think if he could at least do that much, we could get through this."

"Mmm-hmm," Sye hummed, unimpressed.

"What?" Torrie challenged.

"So, with all your crying and carrying on, what exactly did you accomplish?"

Torrie grinned, "Six months. Couples therapy. A weekend retreat."

Sye whistled, "Whew! Sounds like you really put in work."

"I did," Torrie sat up straighter, her voice softening, "But it wasn't just for show, Sye. I really do want my husband back."

Silence again.

Then, "Alright, well, I don't want to sound like the devil's advocate, but you know I have to ask…"

Torrie held her breath.

"What if he doesn't come around after six months?"

A sharp pain twisted in her stomach.

Her throat closed up.

I don't want to think about that. I can't.

Sye must have sensed her hesitation because her voice softened. "You know what? Let's talk about this later. I've gotta run."

Torrie nodded, swallowing the lump in her throat. "Bye, Sye."

She ended the call and dropped the phone onto the passenger seat.

Torrie closed her eyes.

If anyone could read through her, it was Symeria.

But that was not a question she wanted to answer.

She was getting her husband back.

Whatever it took.

CHAPTER EIGHTEEN

Amari

Three months into this counseling hell, Amari was convinced that fate was out to get him.

If he had lived in any other state, he'd be divorced by now.

But no.

Here in Georgia, the marriage counselor was dragging it out, talking about "rebuilding trust" and "exploring unresolved emotions."

For what?

He had already made up his mind. It was over.

Lucky for him, the judge had only mandated six months before they could file the final papers. If the counselor had their way, they'd be stuck doing this for a damn year.

Damn that.

He wasn't here to be *rehabilitated.* He was here because he *had* to be.

And if Torrie thought six months was going to change his mind, she was fooling herself.

⁂

Amari *knew* he made things worse for himself when the counselor asked if he had ever strayed outside of the marriage, and he shot back with:

"Before or after I found out she cheated?"

Torrie's face had dropped.

The *look* she gave him was priceless, but he didn't care.

She needed to sit with that. Let it burn.

The counselor, though? Not amused.

She called his response a *deflection tactic* and said they had "issues to unpack."

Then, just because his life wasn't miserable enough, she upped their sessions from once a week to twice.

Twice. A. Week.

Amari should've just kept his mouth shut.

The thing was, Amari didn't have a problem with counseling.

But he was sick and tired of hearing about how they "lacked communication."

How?

They *talked* all the time.

They had plenty of conversations: arguments, debates, even damn near full-blown conferences about their issues.

What more was there to say?

Amari had done his part. He showed up. He listened. He tried.

But sitting through session after session of hearing how much he failed her?

How *he* should've been more adventurous, more open, more exciting.

That was bullshit.

If Torrie wanted to do all the freaky shit she was so curious about, why didn't she just say that?

She didn't need permission.

Instead, she went out and found it somewhere else.

That wasn't on him.

Was he ever going to forgive her?

He didn't know.

But one thing was for sure:

He would never forget.

CHAPTER NINETEEN

Dash

Three months ago, she said it.

And she'd say it again.

She loved Savannah.

It was beautiful. Peaceful. Exactly what she needed.

Yesterday, the weather had been perfect, just enough chill in the air to sit at Lake Mayer and people-watch comfortably without being too cold.

Funny how she used to think sitting in one place, just being still, was a waste of time. Now?

She craved it.

No demands. No rushing. No obligations.

Just living.

Dash chuckled to herself as she thought about Symeria's question the other day.

"Are you planning on getting a job?"

A job?

For what?

Dash had planned too well to need a job.

She wasn't one of those people who got out of the military with no game plan, struggling to figure out what came next.

Nope. She had been preparing for retirement since Day One.

She'd saved. She'd invested. She'd handled her business.

If she worked, it wouldn't be for money. It would be for fun.

Symeria didn't know that, though.

Sye thought Dash had just been a good old' government employee, doing her twenty years and punching the clock.

Absolutely not.

From the moment she left home for Ft. Jackson, South Carolina, Dash had been moving with intention.

And now?

She was set.

Sure, she'd help her sister out if she needed it, just for kicks, but other than that?

It was a chill city for her.

 Trinity Sierra Sesay

A job?

Yeah, right.

⸺◦⧉◦⸺

Dash let the soft breeze brush against her skin as she strolled along the lake, her mind drifting back to childhood.

She and Sye used to play pretend here, holding up their hands like imaginary cameras, *snapping* pictures of their reflections in the water.

Good times.

She smiled at the memory, but her moment of nostalgia was cut short.

Something… felt off.

She wasn't alone.

A man stood across the lake, staring.

Dash froze.

She wasn't the paranoid type, but there was something about him. Something unsettling.

She glanced around. There were plenty of people here.

So why did it feel like he was staring at her?

She didn't recognize him. Never seen him before. But still, something wasn't right.

For the next thirty minutes, he stayed in place, barely moving.

And then, just as smoothly as he had arrived, he turned and walked away.

Dash watched as he climbed into a stealthy black Dodge Charger and disappeared down the road.

She never got close enough to catch his plates.

But that feeling in her gut?

It stayed with her long after he was gone.

CHAPTER TWENTY

Symeria

"Darenda!"

"Yes, Miss Hayes?"

"What time is the company coming to fix my internet?"

"There's a three-hour window, so anywhere between noon and three. Oh, and the Network Security rep is here now."

Sye frowned, *"Network Security rep?"*

Darenda, catching my confusion, added, "The Cyber Security guy. You said you wanted to look into other security options after that ransomware attack on the City's servers last month."

Ah. That.

Sometimes, Darenda spoke so fast that I needed a minute to process what she was saying.

"So, I scheduled a rep to come speak with you," she continued.

She sighed, "Darenda, when I said that, I was thinking out loud. I don't remember actually asking you to do this."

"Oh…" a brief pause, "Well… I thought that was what you wanted, so I called. He's here now, right outside. Want me to send him away?"

Sye let out a slow breath, shaking her head.

"No. I'll talk to him. Bring him in."

"Got it."

This was going to be a long morning. Sye wasn't in the mood for security jargon, firewall strategies, or corporate sales pitches.

She barely had time to process my last conversation with Dash before her office door swung open again.

Darenda poked her head in.

"Miss Hayes, this is Mr. Adonis Embry."

Sye stood up to be professional, but the moment she saw him, her face betrayed her.

She could feel it, her lips stretching into a full, tooth-showing smile.

Damn.

This man had to be at least six feet tall. Not traditionally handsome, but… tall.

     Trinity Sierra Sesay

"It's nice to meet you, Ms. Hayes," he said, his voice smooth.

She snapped herself back into business mode.

"Nice to meet you as well, Mr. Embry," she gestured toward the chair, "Please, have a seat."

As he sat, she decided to set clear boundaries for this meeting upfront.

"Let me just say this: I'm not making an instant purchase."

Adonis arched an eyebrow, intrigued.

"I like to research before committing to anything," I continued, "So, no haggling, no statistic-dropping, no aggressive sales tactics. Just show me what you have, leave me some literature, and wait for my call."

He smirked.

"Noted," he leaned back, studying her, "Am I allowed to ask questions, or is that against the rules too?"

A chuckle slipped out before she could stop it.

"Questions are allowed," she admitted.

The meeting went smoother than she expected. She explained her concerns, and Adonis offered practical suggestions without the usual sales fluff. He left her with a few brochures and a promise to follow up in a week.

As she watched him leave, she had the strangest craving.

Pralines.

Why?

No idea.

But if she wanted the best, she'd have to go downtown, near the river.

Ugh. Downtown Savannah.

Abercorn was basically the only way in, the only way out, and those damn traffic squares, one after another, were hell.

Yes, yes, historic charm and all that.

But all she saw was traffic.

She sighed and decided to scrap the idea. Maybe she'd just make something at home instead. Torrie might be up to it.

It'd be good for her, a distraction from everything.

Most days, she just sulked around the house, working when she had to, mourning her marriage in silence.

For the past three months, having both Dash and Torrie living with her had felt like college again except this time, they weren't surviving on ramen and off-brand cereal.

Surprisingly, they hadn't argued once. No sideways conversations, no petty fights, no spilled secrets, thanks to Dash's questionable moral compass.

She still couldn't believe the scene between her and Amari.

 Trinity Sierra Sesay

Dash was so… unbothered about sex. No emotional attachment. No guilt. Just sex.

If Torrie ever found out? She'd be devastated.

But worse than that?

If she found out Sye knew.

Because she did.

And she kept it from her.

Sye took a deep breath, shaking off the thought.

Torrie missed Amari. Despite the separation, she wanted to reconcile.

But how do you fix a marriage when two people won't even talk?

And Dash?

She was a mystery of her own. She never let anyone phase her.

She got approached all the time, but she kept men at arm's length, like relationships weren't even an option.

She just seemed so… content.

But was she?

Or was she just avoiding something?

CHAPTER TWENTY-ONE

Amari

Who in the hell does she think she is?

Sitting in that therapist's office, spewing lies, telling some half-baked story about how her infidelity had everything to do with what he would or wouldn't do in bed.

Typical.

Typical of women.

Instead of owning up to their own damn mistakes, they twist the truth into something convenient. A blame game. And Torrie thought she was playing it well until he shut that shit down.

The second she tried to paint him as the reason for her affair, Amari cut her off.

"If I'm so sexually dysfunctional, then wouldn't I actually have to be trying to have sex… with you?" he fired back.

That one hit.

Her face fell.

She bought it.

Good.

Let her feel the same gut-wrenching pain he had felt when he found out she was riding another man.

Let that image live in her head now.

The truth?

Aside from that one time with Dash, which, in his mind, was just therapy, he hadn't been with anyone else.

But she didn't need to know that.

Let her wonder.

Let her think he had someone else.

Because now? Now, she would know exactly what it felt like to question everything. To obsess over the possibilities. To picture him laying with another woman the way she laid with that bastard.

Hell, maybe she'd even lose sleep over it.

He had just made it crystal clear that his lack of effort in bed wasn't because he lacked creativity.

It was because she wasn't a factor anymore.

Sex with her? It wasn't passion. It wasn't love.

     Trinity Sierra Sesay

It was a chore.

And he was done doing chores.

Amari leaned back in his chair, fuming as he stared at the ceiling.

What the hell would she pull next week?

At this point, therapy was pointless.

He didn't want to be here. Didn't want to hear her voice trying to justify what she did.

Didn't want to see her face when she cried about a marriage she destroyed.

He wanted to be done.

With her.

With this joke of a process.

With every trace of what they used to be.

CHAPTER TWENTY-TWO

Dash

For the past week, Dash's phone had been blowing up with calls from an unfamiliar number.

No voicemails.

No messages.

Just rings.

Every time she ignored it, they'd hang up and call again like a persistent bill collector.

This time, she was in the shower when it started up again, the same back-to-back calls.

Not Symeria. She was still in bed.

Not Torrie. She was watching TV.

She was tired of guessing.

With water dripping down her arm, she snatched the phone off the counter and answered with irritation simmering in her voice.

"Hello?"

Silence.

"Hello!" she snapped, louder this time.

Then it came.

A low, deep chuckle slid through the speaker, making her skin prickle.

"Tsk, tsk, tsk…Sylena, now don't you know how rude it is to answer the phone shouting at people?"

That voice.

That damn voice.

Dash exhaled sharply through her nose, gripping the phone tighter.

Robert.

Again.

"Yep, it's me," he confirmed as if reading her mind.

"I told you that you wouldn't be able to get away from me."

She rolled her eyes so hard that it almost hurt. Here we go.

"I fully plan on making you pay for what you did," he continued, his voice calm but sharp. Too calm.

    Trinity Sierra Sesay

Dash's pulse quickened slightly, but she refused to let him hear it in her voice.

"Why can't you understand that until you face me, deal with me, and give me what I want…

…you will have no peace?"

The words slithered through the line like a threat dipped in honey.

Just as she parted her lips to respond…

Click.

Call ended.

Dash glared at the blank screen.

Coward.

She tried calling back, but unlisted number.

Of course.

She tossed the phone onto the counter and stared at herself in the mirror, gripping the edge of the sink.

What the hell did he even want?

He was talking like she had wronged him, like he was owed something.

Like she was supposed to be afraid.

But if Robert thought he could rattle her, he was in for a rude awakening.

Dash smirked.

She had handled bigger threats than him.

If he wanted chaos, he was messing with the right one.

Men.

CHAPTER TWENTY-THREE

Taureen

Two days and six hours later, Torrie was still seething over what Amari had said.

He couldn't possibly believe that she thought he had an affair, could he?

Was that his goal?

To hurt her the way she hurt him?

If so, he succeeded.

Torrie wasn't stupid.

She knew exactly what he was doing: weaponizing his words. And Amari's words? They could cut deeper than a knife.

She clenched her jaw.

He knew words hurt.

And yet, he said them anyway.

Torrie loved her husband…

But she didn't enjoy making love to him.

That was the ugly truth.

She wasn't sure if she ever truly had.

Now, sitting across from him in another excruciating therapy session, she watched him hang onto every word the therapist spoke.

Everything she asked?

He answered.

Everything she suggested?

He listened.

His body was relaxed, his expression open.

Then, the moment the conversation shifted to her.

His entire face changed.

His shoulders tensed.

His lips pressed together.

And the disgust in his eyes?

Unmistakable.

It was like she was just another case file to be closed.

Not his wife.

Not the woman he once adored.

It wasn't that she thought Amari had some secret attraction to their therapist, but the way he gave her respect, attention…

The way he used to look at her?

That stung the most.

Marriage was supposed to be for better or for worse.

And yet…

Here they were.

He wasn't trying.

He wasn't fighting for them.

He wasn't even angry anymore.

He was just…done.

Torrie swallowed hard and stared at her lap.

She didn't know if she should start thinking about moving on now…

Or just put it off until later.

But something had to change.

Jarrod.

His name slithered into her mind before she could stop it.

Her fingers tightened into fists.

Even with everything that was falling apart around her, he kept popping up in her head, taking up space he didn't deserve.

She told herself she didn't have feelings for him.

But if that were true…

Why was she still thinking about him?

It wasn't just the way he listened…

It was the way he kissed her.

Soft. Slow. Intentional.

The way he trailed his lips down her neck, pausing, teasing…

Like she was an instrument he played effortlessly, composing a song only they could hear.

That's how it started.

And that's how it always ended.

One. Random. Kiss. At a time.

Torrie sucked in a sharp breath and snapped out of it when she heard Dash yelling at her phone.

Her stomach twisted.

What the hell was wrong with her?

She was on the verge of losing the only man she had ever truly loved.

The one who had accepted her, flaws and all.

And yet…

Instead of thinking about fighting for her marriage,

She was reliving stolen moments with the man who had helped destroy it.

The man who had made her break her vows.

The man who had ruined everything.

No.

She had ruined everything.

CHAPTER TWENTY-FOUR

Dash

Dash flipped a page of the newspaper as she ignored her phone ringing for the fifth time in a row. She wasn't in the mood to entertain him today, plus it was getting old. If this was his idea of making her miserable, he was doing a terrible job at it, she thought.

She messed up his life? He did it on his own. Dash didn't see why she was being attacked because of his slimy behavior. All this started when that woman showed up, making accusations about her that weren't true. She tried to tell this woman that it wasn't what it seemed. Her perception of her was all wrong. She was not a homewrecker and had never been one. Dash didn't know that he was married. For over eight months, he was a single man with no ties. She never saw evidence of a wife, not at his home, not in his car, his hand bared no ring, so how was she supposed to know?

In eight months, they went out a multitude of times, always seen in the public with his friends and hers. No one knew about his double life. That's what happens when you are a geographical bachelor. His wife lived in Memphis, and she visited every now and then. Dash only found out he was married when his wife paid her a visit.

Dash glanced up from her desk as the door to her office creaked open. A civilian woman stood in the doorway, looking hesitant but determined.

"Master Sergeant Hayes?" she asked.

Dash sat up a little, eyeing the unfamiliar face. Civilians didn't just waltz onto base, and when they did, it was usually for something serious.

"That's me," Dash confirmed, setting her pen down, "And you are?"

The woman stepped inside cautiously, clasping her hands together.

The woman took a careful step forward, "Juliette Roberts."

Dash looked at her as if her whole being was saying, "And?" so she repeated herself, "I'm Julie Jaspers, Robert, Jaspers' wife!"

Dash guessed when there was no expression on her face; the woman took the hint that she had no clue who she was talking about. So, she opened her pocketbook, pulled out her phone, and showed a picture of her and him. It was Keith, Keith Roberts, actually known as Robert Keith Jaspers.

"You look surprised," she said curtly, but something in her tone led Dash to believe that her words were sincere. She was more than surprised, more like blown away, but what she was feeling on the inside was not resonating well on the outside; this was obvious. Dash looked up from the picture and just stared at her for a few seconds before she got up from her desk and walked over to the door to close it. The woman's facial expression showed her puzzlement at Dash's height and stature. Being tall was one thing, but when you had a presence that showed, it could be intimidating, and that was what Dash was aiming for. After closing the door and sitting back down in her seat, she looked her in the eyes. *She was pretty*, Dash thought, and *a little curvy. Her dimples were definitely an asset.*

"You said that you wanted to talk ...talk." Dash was calm in her response. The kind of calm that had developed from her years in the military.

The woman looked as if she didn't know what to say or where to start. It's funny, in your mind, the plan always sounds like a good one and then when you go to execute it, not so much. Dash watched her search for words as if she didn't really know where to start or what to say, and then finally, she said it, she asked the one question all women who have been cheated on want to know: "Why?"

Dash curtly said, "Why what?"

At that point, reality stepped in, and the woman realized that the 'weak-hearted woman' appeal was not going to work with her, so she sat up straight, looked Dash in the eye, and said, "Why were you having an affair with my husband?"

Dash leaned back in her chair and repositioned her body while she thought about how she wanted to answer. It would have been easy for her to snap back harshly, but the truth was, she didn't want to. For some reason, she really wanted to have this conversation.

"You are assuming that I knew that he was "A" husband." Dash made sure to place an emphasis on the "A" as well as supporting it with an air quote as a hand gesture.

"Are you saying that you didn't?"

"No, actually, I didn't."

"I don't understand," she said with a puzzled look on her face, "He wears a wedding ring. Our pictures are all over his apartment; how could you not know?"

⎯⎯⎯❧⎯⎯⎯

"I'm confused," Dash said, "you want to know why I had an affair with your husband, or how did I not know he was your husband? Which one?"

"Ms. Hayes. I am just trying to get to the bottom of this situation. I'm not happy with knowing my husband has been sleeping with another woman, a homewrecker. As a woman, I was hoping that I could appeal to you to stop. You have to understand that this is not easy for me at all."

Dash looked at her, and she could see the hurt in her eyes, but the one thing that she did not see was rage or anger, and that puzzled her.

"How did you find out about us?" Dash said in a very short manner.

The woman looked at her for what seemed like an eternity as if something within her had awakened her. She gave her this piercing look as if to say, *you really want to know?* "My husband said your name while sleeping and holding me in his arms. I didn't think anything of it at first. I thought he was dreaming about a dog or something," she said snidely, "but then the next night, while making love, he said it again in a whisper. He doesn't even realize what he did or said as I have not questioned him about it, but between that and the nasty things that he has wanted to do sexually, lately, I knew there was a whore involved."

"Ok," Dash said as she crossed her legs, leaning back in her chair, "Let me be very clear: what's your name again? Julie? It's one thing for you to come up in my office without warning, but if you think for one second you are going leave the same way you came with continued insults, you are delusional. My advice to you is, pick your battles, or this conversation is over."

She blinked and then apologized, "I really don't know what I was expecting to accomplish by coming here. Part of me wants answers and I really do believe that I envisioned something quite different. I was looking for a fight, an argument, something, but that's not what you are giving me and I guess I don't understand why or what's happening. So, Dash, please forgive me, but I am truly in unchartered waters here."

"Ok, so he called out my name while you were having sex; how did that lead to you finding me?"

Juliette exhales sharply, gripping the edge of her seat, "At first, I wasn't sure I heard it right. I wanted to believe I was imagining things. But the way he froze? The way he tried to cover it up?" (She shakes her head.) "I knew."

Dash raises an eyebrow but says nothing.

"The next morning, I waited until he was asleep and went through his phone."

Dash tilts her head, "That's bold."

(ignoring the comment) "I found messages. Deleted ones. And pictures of you. Screenshots of your social media, old texts."

Dash keeps her expression neutral, but inside, she's calculating.

"So, I did what any woman in my position would do. I looked you up. I found your name, your rank, and your unit. And then I came here."

Dash lets out a slow breath, tapping her fingers against the desk.

"All that, just to look me in the face?" Dash said.

Juliet meeting her gaze "No".

A beat of silence.

"I came to hear the truth. From you."

Now Dash was feeling it, compassion. The woman was no friend of hers, but she could truly identify with where she was coming from. She wanted answers, but she didn't know what questions to ask.

Dash took a deep breath and started from the beginning, "I met him at the gym; he was using the stair climber next to mine. I had on a necklace that he found interesting, and we started talking about it, then other things. It was just a thirty-minute conversation. After I got off, I left. It was three weeks before I saw him again in the gym. So again, we started talking; it was no big deal, he wasn't on my radar, and I wasn't on his, I don't think. A couple of days after that, we ran into each other at a club. We started talking, and the next thing you know, there was a dinner, and phone calls, pop-up visits, then dates."

Everything had been so magical. He was such a gentleman, she thought as she stared at the woman before her. Keith hadn't pushed the issue of sex, and that was great. At the time, Dash wasn't looking for anyone to be in her life. Her focus was on retiring, and then she met him. They had such a vast knowledge of each other that it was almost like they were born together.

Dash knew she wanted to ask questions, but she didn't; she just listened. "I always look for a ring or evidence of one, but there weren't any. He didn't have one on the first day I met him; I remembered because I looked. After going out a couple of times, we started meeting each other's friends and stopping by each other's office. We were very open. Everyone knew we were dating, and no one posed any pushback or offense to it."

Dash wasn't sure how much to share with her, so she paused, and Keith's wife asked the question Dash knew she wanted to know all along... "When did you have sex with him?"

"It was in our third month of dating. We went away for the weekend, and we made love on the balcony of our hotel in the Poconos, overlooking the beach."

The first time they made love, Dash had thought she was in the midst of a soap opera or something. She recalled taking a walk on the beach, and the moon was aglow. It was a reddish color, setting over the ocean. They were on the balcony; he held her around the waist and kissed her on her neck. The twinge of the kiss resonated down Dash's back and legs. He kissed her again softly, and she felt her womanhood start to pulsate. His hands then rubbed against her thighs, up to the top of her thong, and then, in one swoop, he slipped them off and allowed them to drop to the floor. He turned Dash around to face him. His lips kept in contact with her body, first her neck, then her shoulders, her breast, her nipples; he made his way down to her space.

The taping of the woman's foot brought her out of her reverie. His wife was beginning to fidget. Her body was moving steadily as she tapped her foot continuously.

"What about his apartment? Have you been there? Didn't you see the pictures of us?"

Dash just swallowed before speaking and politely said, "I have been to his apartment on several occasions. Slept over

 Trinity Sierra Sesay

many times and at one point had a key and there were never any pictures."

The tears were welling up in her eyes, and then she jumped up and ran to the door. Before the woman opened it, she yelled, "You're a whore and a liar. Stay away from my husband!" She opened the door and quickly walked, almost running out of the building.

Dash was glad the soldiers were on break. The last thing she needed today was to have her colleagues and soldiers hear that she was a whore.

CHAPTER TWENTY-FIVE

Symeria

I don't know which is worse.

The damn copier or the damn computer network.

Both were betraying me today.

Sye was sick of it.

"Darenda!" she yelled, rubbing her temples.

As usual, she appeared perky as ever.

"Yes, Miss Hayes? What's wrong?"

", is out again."

She sighed, "Here, let me see if I can fix it."

"There's no time for that," Sye cut her off, "Please just call the network people about the firewall issues and get the maintenance guy in for the copier."

She exhaled sharply as she nodded and left the room.

Thankfully, the network technician showed up within the hour.

One problem down.

The copier, however,?

Still dead.

Sye was lost in a daydream, halfway considering a new career in a profession where machines didn't betray you, when she heard the front door open.

She remembered that Darenda was still out at lunch.

She sighed, pushed her chair back, and called out, "I'll be right there!"

Expecting Carl, the copier maintenance guy, she walked toward the front.

And stopped short.

It wasn't Carl.

It was Adonis.

The Cyber Security rep.

"Adonis?" she blinked, caught off guard, "Hi. What are you doing here?"

"You look startled," he said, grinning, "Did I catch you at a bad time? I apologize if I did."

"No, I'm sorry," she recovered quickly, "I didn't mean to look that way. I was expecting the copier maintenance tech."

"Oh, I understand," he nodded, glancing around, "So, your copier is out?"

She folded her arms, "Yep."

"Would you like me to take a look at it?"

She hesitated.

Adonis… fixing a copier?

She squinted at him, "You know how to fix copiers?"

He chuckled, "It's not that complicated. Machines have logic. Computers, printers, copiers: same principles."

She wasn't sure how true that was, but before she could respond, he added,

"No charge."

She raised an eyebrow, "No charge?"

He smiled, "I'm here, might as well."

Something about his grin made her slightly uneasy, but she couldn't quite pinpoint why.

Still, she found herself saying, "Sure, okay. If you want."

She led him to the back office, where the evil copier sat in its useless glory.

He rolled up his sleeves and took it apart piece by piece, handling everything delicately.

Then, suddenly:

"Ah-ha."

She frowned, "What does 'ah-ha' mean?"

Adonis smirked, "Your bulb is out."

He pointed to a roller thing inside, "And this? This part that actually copies the documents? It's cracked."

She sighed deeply.

Of course.

"So…" she crossed her arms, "Let me guess, you want to fix it now, don't you?"

He shook his head, laughing, "Actually, no."

She raised a brow, "No?"

"I said I'd look at it, and I did," his eyes twinkled mischievously.

He was messing with me.

"Oh," she smirked, "so you're a wise guy now, huh?"

"No wiser than you, Miss 'Yes, you can ask A question.'"

She burst out laughing.

Okay, that was a good comeback.

He had gotten her back.

After their laughter died down, he leaned against the desk.

"The copier can be fixed," he said, "but it'll probably be expensive."

She sighed again.

"So, here's what I suggest," he continued, "Let your guy take a look at it. If the cost is too high, give me a call. I have a guy."

She raised an eyebrow, "You have a guy?"

He grinned, "I always have a guy."

She chuckled, "Good to know."

They walked back to the front, and as she opened the door for him, she suddenly remembered.

"Oh! Why did you stop by?"

He smiled, "Just following up. Wanted to see if you had read the literature I left you."

She gave him a knowing look, "A follow-up visit, huh?"

"Of course," he smirked, "That's what good sales-people do."

She shook my head, laughing softly.

"See you soon, Ms. Hayes," he said, stepping out the door.

She watched him leave.

Still grinning.

CHAPTER TWENTY-SIX

Amari

Their homework assignment from the counselor was simple:

Write a letter to each other.

There were only three rules:

1. Write from the heart.
2. Be honest.
3. Do not say anything negative about the other person.

Amari wasn't sure what this was supposed to resolve.

But if it got him closer to being free?

So. Be. It.

————

Dear Taureen,

That is your name, right?

I'm just asking because I don't know who you are anymore, so I'm not quite sure what to call you.

Anyway.

The only reason I'm taking the time to write this letter is because I am ready to be rid of you.

And this is apparently the fastest and only way to do that.

Writing from the heart—*check.*

Being honest—*check.*

Not saying anything negative about you, Taureen—*check.*

If that is who you really are.

Amari

 Trinity Sierra Sesay

CHAPTER TWENTY-SEVEN

Taureen

Torrie lay sprawled across her bed when she heard Sye come home.

She loved the way her friend always made her way upstairs to check on her and Dash if they weren't in the living room.

Just like a momma bear.

Sye cared.

She had always cared.

Before she could even say hi, Torrie blurted out:

"Sye, Amari's antics are getting old! Do you know this fool wrote me a letter questioning my name? Like we just met or something? Counseling is supposed to help, but all it's done is give him an excuse to be cruel. And for him, the crueler, the better."

"Wow, Torrie."

Sye walked toward the bedroom, and brows furrowed with concern.

She sat at the edge of the bed and sighed.

"I thought after five months of counseling and separation, you two would have made some progress. Is he even trying?"

Torrie scoffed.

"No. It's like being cruel, mean, and demeaning is empowering him. I have never," she shook her head, "I would have never in my wildest of wildest dreams thought this man would act like this."

Sye reached over and wrapped her arms around her, pulling her into a hug.

"I don't know, Torrie. It's unfortunate, and I hate to say this, but maybe you should start thinking about life without Amari. I know that's hard to hear, but this may be your reality."

Torrie wanted to cry.

But she just couldn't.

Sye was right.

It was time to get with the program.

She was soon to be the ex-wife of Mr. Amari Conteh.

And she needed to start wrapping her head around it.

CHAPTER TWENTY-EIGHT

Symeria

After years of dealing with that old copier, Sye finally decided to ditch it for a new multifunction printer. It was long overdue. She nearly gave birth to a duck when Carl, the maintenance guy, confirmed what Adonis had already pointed out: *the repair would cost me her three thousand dollars. Three. Thousand. Dollars.* At that point, she didn't even bother calling Adonis for his "guy." It wasn't about being cheap, she just wasn't about to throw away money fixing something older than some of her employees.

On top of that, she finally upgraded her office's network security system. Given the cyberattacks the city had experienced, she wasn't about to take any chances. Protecting her clients' data was non-negotiable, and she refused to be one of those businesses caught slipping.

When the tech team arrived, she was excited to see a group of badass Black women running the installation. But, she won't lie, she was a little disappointed that Adonis wasn't with them.

Why? No idea. It wasn't like he worked in tech installation. But still… wishful thinking.

The truth was, she actually wanted to see him again. She couldn't explain it, but there was something about him, a quiet giant wrapped in a mountain of muscle.

She was lost in thought when one of the techs asked her to sign off on their work. She waved them toward Darenda, who handled it like the boss she was. Then she slipped back into her office and shut the door.

⸺⧯⧯⧯⸺

Three Weeks Later

There was a gentle knock at her office door. Then she heard a familiar voice.

"Symeria?"

She recognized it instantly. Adonis.

She jumped up, almost too excited, then caught herself and smoothed down her dress, hoping he didn't notice.

"Adonis," she stuttered, trying to sound casual, "What are you doing here?"

He smiled nervously, and for some reason, that made her stomach tighten.

"I was in the neighborhood and thought I'd check in to see how the new network security is treating you," then he

 Trinity Sierra Sesay

brought his hand from behind his back, revealing a bouquet of deep purple tulips.

"Oh my God, these are gorgeous!" she gasped, bringing them close to her nose, "Purple tulips are my absolute favorite. How did you know?"

"A little bird told me," he grinned.

Out of the corner of her eye, she caught movement behind him. Darenda was standing off to the side, trying to be discreet. Too late. Busted.

"That little bird wouldn't happen to be named Darenda, would it?"

"Maybe," he admitted, his smile widening.

Darenda, knowing she was caught, scurried forward and snatched the bouquet from her hands. "I'll put these in water," she said quickly before vanishing.

She shook her head, laughing under her breath.

"So, how's the network?" Adonis asked, looking around her office like he actually cared.

"It's great," she said, "No issues so far."

"Good. Do you need anything?"

"Nope, I think we're covered," I said, trying to sound professional, but my voice came out a little too clipped.

She couldn't help but admire him. Beige slacks, a lavender pinstripe shirt, and a perfectly coordinated purple, green, and beige tie. The man knew how to put himself together. And then there was his scent. Clean. Crisp. Expensive. She knew that smell.

"Wait..." she tilted my head, "Is that Bvlgari?"

His smile deepened, "It is. Are you a fan?"

"Yes, I love the smell. It's fresh, not too overpowering."

"My sister gave it to me for Christmas last year, and I've been wearing it ever since."

"She has good taste," she said.

They stood there for a moment, just looking at each other. The energy between them was unmistakable.

"Well," he said, shifting slightly, "I guess I should get going. I'm glad everything's working fine. Just let me know if you ever need anything."

Something inside her screamed not to let him leave.

She swallowed, then blurted out, "Before you go, can I ask you something?"

He stopped and turned back to her, curious, "Sure. Let me guess, you need more reading materials, you want to upgrade?"

She laughed, "No, nothing like that." She hesitated, then took a breath, "I was just wondering... is there a Mrs. Adonis?"

He blinked, then chuckled, rubbing the back of his neck, "No, no Mrs. Adonis."

"Okay," she nodded, "How about a significant other?"

"Nope," he said, his smile softening.

They locked eyes again. She had opened this door, so she had to walk through it.

"Would it be too forward of me to ask you out for drinks sometime?" I asked, biting my lip slightly.

His smile widened as he took a small step closer. "Not forward at all," he said, lowering his voice, "But there is one thing…"

She felt my stomach flip, "What's that?"

He grinned, "I don't drink."

They both laughed.

"Dinner, then?" she suggested.

"Dinner would be good," he agreed.

They exchanged numbers, and as soon as he walked out the door, she practically jumped out of her skin with excitement.

⸺⸺

Later That Night

When she got home, she couldn't wait to tell Dash and Torrie. For once, they were all home at the same time: a rare occurrence these days.

As soon as she walked in, she dropped her purse on the counter, "You girls are not going to believe what just happened!"

Dash arched a brow, "Ooooh, do tell."

She flopped onto the couch, grinning like a fool, "So, you remember Adonis, the cyber security guy?"

Torrie gasped, "Girl, don't tell me…"

"Yes," she cut in, "We have a date coming Friday."

They both squealed like teenagers.

"You mean fine-ass, broad-shouldered Adonis?" Dash teased.

She laughed, "Yes, that one."

Torrie clapped her hands, "Okay, so what are you wearing?"

She groaned, "That's the problem. Girls, I need your help. I want to look…"

"Stunning," Dash finished for her.

"Yes."

Dash cracked her knuckles, "Say no more. I got you."

And just like that, Operation Look Unforgettable for Adonis was officially in motion.

 Trinity Sierra Sesay

CHAPTER TWENTY-NINE

Amari & Taureen

Amari positioned himself at the far end of the couch, as far away from his wife as possible. The couch wasn't that large, so even with the distance, they were still within arm's reach. He had been careful not to look at Taureen since the session began, but he could feel her eyes on him, studying him.

She finally spoke, "Amari, I thought the whole point of counseling was to work things out."

"No, Taureen," he said, his voice measured, calm, but edged with ice, "The whole point of counseling is to convince the therapist that you're a whore who cheated on her husband so she can sign off on this divorce."

Taureen felt the words like a slap across the face. She barely managed to keep her composure. Who was this man? The Amari sitting across from her was unrecognizable.

"Dr. Apara, this can't possibly be fair," her voice shook as she turned toward their counselor, *"He's allowed to say these things to me while you just sit there?"*

Dr. Apara, ever composed, pushed her glasses up the bridge of her nose and glanced at her notes. "Amari, I understand that emotions are running high, but I'm going to ask that you tone it down. This is supposed to be a space for constructive communication, not verbal attacks."

Amari leaned back, crossing his arms over his chest, "Fine."

Dr. Apara turned toward him, "Now, Amari, why do you feel that your wife is a 'whore'?"

"That's easy," he said without hesitation, "She had sex with a man who wasn't her husband."

"And that's the only reason?"

"Yes."

She tilted her head, "Are you sure?"

Amari hesitated, his jaw tightening.

Taureen recognized that look; he was on the defensive now. The therapist had backed him into a corner.

After a beat, Amari exhaled sharply, "Okay... no. There's more."

This time, his voice was lower. Controlled. Almost too calm.

"She didn't just cheat," he said, his eyes locking onto hers for the first time in the session, "She told me, she blamed me, said she had the affair because I wasn't satisfying her sexually."

Taureen's breath hitched. This was it. This was the root of his rage.

Amari turned back to the therapist, his tone clipped but firm, "That's a cop-out. That's cowardly. Why not just own up to it?" He turned back to her, his gaze burning, "Just say you did what you did because that's what you wanted to do. Don't put it on me."

Dr. Apara let the room settle before speaking, "Amari, how did it feel hearing that from Taureen?"

He swallowed hard, and for the first time in months, his eyes softened. He clenched his jaw, fighting something back.

"Pain," his voice was barely above a whisper, "It felt like she had taken a knife and cut me wide open while I was alive and able to feel every bit of it."

The room was silent except for the faint ticking of the office clock.

Dr. Apara looked at Taureen, "Taureen, it looks like you want to respond."

"I do," she sat forward, gripping her hands together, "I tried to explain this to him before, but he wouldn't listen."

"Well," the doctor said gently, "maybe now is the time. Amari, are you ready to listen?"

Amari nodded, his expression unreadable.

"Go ahead, Taureen."

She exhaled slowly. This was her moment.

"I never said Amari didn't satisfy me," she shook her head, "That's not what I meant at all. I was trying to tell him that I wanted to explore more. I wanted us to try new things and new experiences. But whenever I tried to talk to him about it, he brushed me off. When I tried to introduce something new, he ignored it. One night, I went all out, heels, a lace bodysuit, a wig, the whole nine. You know what he did?" Her voice cracked, "He laughed. Laughed. Told me, "Isn't it a little early for Halloween?"

She bit her lip, shaking her head at the memory, "That hurt. I wanted a sexual adventure, and I wanted it with my husband. But what do you do when the person you love won't even try?"

Dr. Apara turned back to Amari, "Amari, your response?"

He clenched his fists, "So, instead of talking to me again, you just found some other guy and slept with him?"

Torrie shook her head, "I did talk to you. I kept trying to talk to you. But you never listened. I never went looking for someone else, Amari. It just… happened."

Silence.

Dr. Apara finally spoke, "This is what I hear from both of you: Taureen, you were looking for something different. The affair itself wasn't just about sex; it was the thrill, the change, the unknown. And Amari, you believed that because you were married, you should have been enough. That alone should have been all the excitement she needed."

Neither of them spoke.

She smiled slightly, "I think we've reached a breakthrough."

Amari scoffed, but it was half-hearted.

Dr. Apara leaned forward, "For your next assignment, I want you both to write another letter to each other. Same rules: from the heart, honest, no negativity. But this time, start your letter with 'If I could…' and complete the sentence."

Neither of them said a word, but they both knew one thing: this wasn't over.

CHAPTER THIRTY

Symeria

Tonight marked one month since Adonis and Sye started seeing each other, and honestly, she was stunned at how much she was enjoying him.

Adonis was different, a good different. He was thoughtful, educated, ambitious, God-fearing, and well-versed in so many things. But the real shocker? The day she surprised him at work with lunch, she found out that he didn't just work for the company; he owned it.

She had been under the impression that he was just another corporate guy in cybersecurity, but he was the CEO. He smiled at her surprise and thanked her for the lunch, impressed by her thoughtfulness but even more surprised that she had been the one to ask him out first.

Sye won't lie; when she first suggested going out, she didn't expect things to get serious. She remember thinking he wasn't particularly aggressive about dating, so she made the first move and asked him out. She was surprised when he said yes, but even more surprised when he took charge of the date like he had been the one to ask her. When she asked about the plan, all he said was, 'I'll text you the address; meet me there.'

That was it. No hints, no buildup.

She wasn't sure what to make of that, but when the night arrived and he finally sent the address, she wasn't thrilled; she was concerned. She remember forwarding the location to Torrie before heading out because, let's be real, women have to be careful these days.

When she plugged the address into her GPS, she realized he had chosen the African Cultural Heritage Museum.

Well… that was different.

She parked and started walking toward the entrance, still trying to process it, when she saw him standing there, tall, confident, and looking way too good in navy-blue slacks and a fitted body shirt. A Tiger Eye necklace with an Ankh pendant sat perfectly on his chest.

He hugged her warmly. Not a side hug, not a hesitant hug, just the right mix of familiar and respectful.

"You look beautiful," he said.

She smiled, but she didn't want to seem too giddy, so she changed the subject. "A museum?"

"Yes," he said, sliding his hands into his pockets, "They feature emerging Black artists every month. This month's theme is Black Photography in Motion."

Okay… now she was impressed.

"Alright, let's do it."

That night was magical.

The exhibits were stunning. The dinner afterwards was well thought out. And when the night seemed to be winding down, he suggested we take a walk by the river.

That's when she really started falling for him.

Talking to Adonis was so easy. She never had to wonder if he was being real; he just was. No games. No pretenses. Just good energy.

We had so much in common, both small business owners, both HBCU grads, and both love to travel. And the real kicker? They were both obsessed with football.

Now, she never thought she'd willingly keep company with a Giants fan, but here they were. And despite the obvious team rivalry (because, "How 'bout dem Cowboys!"), she could already tell football season was going to be interesting.

The only downside? Work.

By the time the season really got going, she was usually drowning in business and barely had time to watch the games. But with Adonis, she had a feeling she'd make the time.

So, when he told her this morning to be ready at 6:30 sharp for our one-month anniversary, she was intrigued.

Most men don't even think about one-month anniversaries, yet here he was, planning something special.

The man. My man.

At least, in her head.

They hadn't actually defined anything yet, but they spent as much time together as they could, considering they were both entrepreneurs with hectic schedules. The beauty of it was they understood that.

No unrealistic expectations. No pressure. Just vibes.

They stole time when they could. An hour for lunch during a packed workweek. A morning walk. A quick FaceTime call at night.

Whatever it took to stay connected.

But tonight? Tonight, she was bringing her A-game.

She glanced in the mirror one last time and smiled. This outfit was hitting.

Gray palazzo pants. A white chenille shell. A fitted gray belted jacket with a French collar and silver buttons. Classy. Elegant. Chic.

To top it off? Five-inch gray and purple pumps, purple accessories, and a matching handbag.

Fierce.

As she walked downstairs, she heard whistles and applause.

        Trinity Sierra Sesay

Torrie and Dash being their usual dramatic selves.

"Sye, you look fierce, girl!" Torrie gave me a high five.

Dash smirked, "Yeah, you look doable." She folded her arms, "And if I know men, doing you is exactly what Mr. Wonderful has in mind tonight."

She rolled her eyes. "Nope!" She held up air quotes, "There's not going to be any 'doing' tonight."

They both burst into laughter.

"I'm serious," she insisted, "We've only been seeing each other for thirty days. That is NOT enough time for his hands or anything else to be in my panties."

Dash squinted, "So… if thirty days isn't long enough, how long before you give up the drawers?"

Torrie nodded, "Yeah, how long?"

Sye shrugged, "I don't have a set number of days. I'm not saying sixty or ninety or whatever. I just… I want to be sure. No skeletons. No surprises. Just the right time."

They both rolled their eyes.

"What?" she threw up my hands, "You can't really know someone in a month. Look at Lindsey. We were together for years, and I still didn't see that blindside coming."

Torrie sighed, "Sye, how long has it been since you last had sex?"

She hesitated, "Uh… a minute."

Dash raised an eyebrow, "No, no, how long?"

Torrie crossed her arms, "Specifically."

Sye sighed, "About twenty-three months."

Dead silence.

She glanced at them, already knowing what was coming.

"Twenty-three months?!" Dash's eyes widened.

Torrie gasped, "Girl, what?!"

Sye exhaled, annoyed, "Yes. Twenty-three months. Happy now?"

Dash smirked, "Nah. But you should be."

She frowned, "Why?"

"Because you have the chance to end that two-year dry spell tonight."

Torrie doubled over laughing.

"I'm not fooling with you girls," she muttered, shaking her head.

And just then, the doorbell rang.

Her thirty-day Mr. Wonderful had arrived.

She opened the door, and there he was, fine as ever.

He smiled and leaned in, pressing a soft kiss to her cheek.

"Hi, beautiful."

 Trinity Sierra Sesay

She melted. Slightly.

In his hands was a bouquet of flowers.

She took them, grinning, "These are gorgeous. Thank you."

He smiled, "Are you ready?"

"Yep."

He waved at the girls as he gently ushered Sye out the door.

"Bye, girls!" she called over her shoulder, "Don't wait up!"

CHAPTER THIRTY-ONE

Taureen

Dear Amari,

If I could go back to the moment, I allowed another man into my mind, my thoughts, and my body...

I would still do it.

Not because I don't regret the pain I caused you, but because for the first time in a long time, I felt something I hadn't felt in years: alive.

I know how that must sound to you. Cold. Unforgivable. But the truth is, as much as I love you, our marriage has not been fulfilling for a long time. And if I'm being honest, I don't think it ever was, not completely.

You are a wonderful man, a great husband in so many ways, but not in the ways that mattered most to me. I needed more, and I tried to tell you that. I begged you to see me, to hear me, to understand what I wanted. But you ignored me. You dismissed me. You laughed at me.

So yes, I gave in to something I shouldn't have. But it wasn't just about sex. It was about feeling wanted, desired, and seen.

Could we have fixed it? Maybe. But we didn't. And we won't.

I fought for this marriage. I fought for you. But I will not continue fighting a battle I've already lost.

You want a divorce? Fine. You can have it.

I won't contest it.

I won't beg.

I won't wait for you to see me.

This way, you'll be free to do you, and I'll finally be free to do me.

- Taureen

CHAPTER THIRTY-TWO

Symeria

Adonis had all the qualities of a keeper.

Forty-five minutes into their date, she was already thinking about how good his hands might feel on her skin. There was something about him, his presence, his energy, that made her feel soft, feminine, protected. He didn't have to do much; it was in the way he moved, spoke, and looked at her that made it clear: this was a man.

When he pulled up in front of Cache, one of Savannah's hottest new restaurants, she was stunned. Reservations here had to be made weeks in advance. She had no idea how he pulled this off, but she was impressed.

As the host led them to their table, she caught a whiff of his scent again, the same musk oil blend she'd smelled when he hugged her at her house earlier. It wasn't overpowering, just clean, masculine, and intoxicating.

Lord, help me.

I was going to need every ounce of self-control to keep this evening pure.

The waiter pulled out Sye's chair and laid a napkin in her lap as Adonis took his seat across from her.

That's when she caught him grinning.

"What?" she asked, raising an eyebrow.

He leaned forward slightly, "I was admiring your beauty. Is that okay with you?"

She blushed before she could stop herself. She never blush. But the way he said it so direct, no hesitation, made her stomach do a little flip.

She tried to play it cool, "I love attention, so admire away."

They both laughed, but then the room went quiet.

Suddenly, they were just staring at each other.

His deep brown eyes locked onto hers, and she felt her pulse quicken. It was one of those moments, the kind where you realize you're sitting across from someone who sees you.

She cleared her throat, needing to break the spell, before she jumped across the table.

"So," she started, forcing a casual tone, "Have you eaten here before?"

He leaned back, stretching his long arms. "Nope, first time. You?"

She shook her head, "No, but I've heard the food is amazing."

He smirked, "Amazing, huh?"

"You don't sound convinced."

"I just like to judge for myself," he said, his voice smooth and deep.

"I can respect that."

Before the tension could rise again, the waiter arrived to take their orders. Thank God.

After they had placed their meals, Adonis casually reached across the table and rested his hand over mine.

She froze.

His touch was warm, strong but gentle.

And then he looked her dead in her eyes and said, "Symeria."

Her breath caught in her throat, "Yes?"

His voice dropped even lower, "I have a serious question to ask you."

She swallowed, her mind racing, "Okay… ask."

He exhaled deeply as if preparing for something heavy, "Can we switch seats? I don't like having my back to the door."

She blinked.

Then she rolled her eyes so hard that she saw her childhood.

Adonis burst out laughing, and she smacked his arm, "Boy, you play too much!"

"I'm serious," he chuckled, "I gotta see what's going on at all times."

She shook her head, still laughing as they switched seats. He was so damn charming, it was ridiculous.

From that moment on, the night flowed effortlessly.

They ate, laughed, and talked about everything: his childhood as the only boy with three sisters, his love for art and travel, and the lessons he learned from his parents. He spoke highly of his father's accomplishments, being a veteran and currently a Captain on the local police force, but his tone about him as a father was rather indifferent. But the way he talked about his mother stuck with me. The way he admired her strength, her resilience, her wisdom.

She liked that. A man who respects women is a man who knows how to love one.

By the time they left the restaurant, she wasn't ready for the night to end.

But Adonis? He was a true gentleman.

He walked me to her door, hands in his pockets, that mischievous smile still playing on his lips.

They stood there in comfortable silence, just looking at each other.

    Trinity Sierra Sesay

And Lord knows, if he had asked to come inside, she don't know if she would've had the strength to say no.

But he didn't.

Instead, he took her hand, lifted it to his lips, and kissed it softly.

"I had a wonderful time, Ms. Hayes," he murmured against her skin, "And I pray we can do this again soon."

"Pray!"

Did this man just say pray?

I didn't know if that was his game or his truth, but either way, it was working.

She smiled, trying not to melt right there on my porch.

"I'd like that," she said.

"Good," he whispered, his lips curving into a knowing grin.

Then, with one last lingering look, he walked away.

She let herself inside and leaned against the door, clutching her chest like a fool.

I was in trouble.

Real trouble.

Because for the first time in a long time, she felt something dangerous. Hope.

CHAPTER THIRTY-THREE

Dash

"Well, well, well. If it isn't Dash, or should I say Sylena? Which is it, baby? What do you want daddy to call you?"

Dash slowly folded her newspaper and set it down, never taking her eyes off him.

Keith. Robert. Jasper.

Whatever the hell he was calling himself these days.

Still tall, still handsome, still a damn fool.

"Oh, now you've got jokes?" he smirked.

She leaned back in her chair, tilting her head, "Not jokes, Keith. Just facts. Or is it Robert? Jasper, maybe?" She let the words roll off her tongue slowly, deliberately, "I forget."

His jaw tightened, "Cute."

He stepped forward, and she instinctively slid away. Seeing him in the flesh was confirmation of what she already knew; he was never hers. Just a liar wrapped in a suit of deception.

"Bet you didn't expect to see me."

She exhaled through her nose, unimpressed, "That's where you're wrong. You've called and threatened me enough for me to know you would show up eventually. I just figured it'd be after dark."

Her eyes swept over him, lips curling slightly, "Didn't think your kind could survive in the daylight."

His slow, mocking chuckle sent a ripple of irritation through her, "One thing I'll say about you, Dash. You were always amusing. Amongst... other things."

Before she could stop herself, her eyes narrowed. Even now, looking at Keith's smug expression, Dash could hear her father's voice as if he were right beside her: "You know why I call you Dash, baby girl? Because you're small, sure, but just a little bit of you changes everything. They won't see you coming, but they'll always know you've been there." She smiled to herself. Keith had no idea how right her father had been.

Don't react.

That was what he wanted.

She squared her shoulders instead, speaking evenly, "What do you want, Keith? And why the hell do you have someone following me?"

Keith's smirk vanished, "I don't know what you're talking about."

 Trinity Sierra Sesay

Dash cocked her head, unimpressed, "Oh, cut the bullshit. I know when I'm being watched."

Keith was about to respond when the waitress appeared.

"Would you like to order, sir?"

Dash didn't let him answer, "He's not staying."

The waitress blinked, nodded, and walked away.

Keith chuckled again, shaking his head, "Damn. Cold-blooded."

"Not cold," Dash corrected, "Done."

Her words hit their mark. His jaw twitched.

"I just want to talk," he finally said.

"Then talk."

"Not here. Somewhere... private."

Dash let out a harsh laugh, "Nah, player. I know your kind of 'private.' I'll pass."

Keith exhaled, "I don't mean like that, Dash. I'm serious."

Something in his tone made her pause.

It wasn't his usual cocky bravado.

It was something else.

"Where?" she asked, guarded.

"There's a park down 204. Quiet. Plenty of places to sit."

Dash studied him, eyes scanning for tells. Then, she smiled.

"Mm-mm. We're not doing that."

Keith frowned, "Doing what?"

Dash tapped her manicured nail against the table, "This. You trying to control the setting. Make me more… comfortable." She let her voice drop a little, teasing, "See, Keith. I remember *exactly* what you sound like when you're lying. And right now? You're damn near poetic."

Keith let out an exasperated breath, "Dash, I just want to talk."

"Then talk," she said smoothly, leaning in slightly, "Right here. In public."

Keith clenched his jaw, glancing around. This wasn't what he wanted. He wanted to control the tempo, the energy. But she had it.

"You want to know why I came?" he said, lowering his voice, "I want to know how it happened. How she found out."

Dash smirked, "You mean how your *wife* found out about *us?*"

Keith's nostrils flared, but he stayed silent.

Dash exhaled through her nose, "See, Keith. You spent all that time thinking you were playing me, and the whole time? Your wife was the one running the game."

Keith leaned forward, "You called her."

Dash tilted her head, "You *really* think that?"

"Yes."

Dash's lips curled, but the amusement didn't reach her eyes.

"You want to know how it happened?" she murmured, "Alright then, baby."

She leaned back in her chair.

"Let me tell you a story."

Keith was frozen.

Dash watched him closely, letting every word sink in.

"I did things to her that sound very familiar, don't they?" she murmured, "Things *you* liked. Things you *begged* me for."

Keith's fingers curled into fists.

Dash smirked.

"Your issue is that I am living rent-free in your minds," she let it settle. Then, softer, like a secret, "Every time you're with her, you see me. And every time she's with you?"

She leaned forward, lips parting slightly as she whispered, "She *feels* me."

The waitress returned, "Anything else I can get for you?"

Dash didn't take her eyes off Keith.

She lifted her hand, slow, deliberate, and waved a single finger in the air.

"Check, please."

CHAPTER THIRTY-FOUR

Adonis

Anyone who knows Savannah understands that pollen season is pure hell.

Between the Spanish moss, live oaks, and the city's infamous humidity, it was a never-ending battle. Savannah didn't really do seasons; it just went from hot to hotter, then back to humid as hell.

And this year?

This year had Adonis suffering.

He had never struggled with allergies this badly before, but this season? His eyes burned, his nose stayed clogged, and his head throbbed so intensely that all he wanted to do was lie in bed and suffer in silence.

He wasn't a complainer. He didn't like being fussed over.

But Symeria?

Symeria saw right through him.

That morning, when she called to check on him, he downplayed everything.

"I'm good," he said, even though his voice was hoarse as hell.

There was a pause. The kind that told him she didn't believe a damn word he just said.

"Did you take anything?"

"No," he admitted, "I don't like medicine. I'll just wait it out."

The silence on the other end? Dangerous.

"Uh-huh," she finally said, "Let's see how waiting it out works for you."

Adonis thought that was the end of it.

Forty-five minutes later, he was proven dead wrong.

There was a knock at the door. When he opened it, there she was, standing with one bag in each hand.

In her right hand: A drugstore bag.

In her left hand: A takeout bag from one of his favorite restaurants.

She raised both bags, achingly unimpressed.

"Here's to your 'I'll just wait it out,' Mr. Embry."

      Trinity Sierra Sesay

He stared at her, caught between surprise and amusement, as she stepped inside like she owned the place.

Inside the drugstore bag? Allergy meds, nasal spray, and eye drops.

Inside the takeout bag? Fresh bagels and hot soup.

Adonis didn't even know what to say.

He didn't ask for this. He didn't expect this.

But I had thought about him.

She showed up.

She paid attention.

And something about that? Hit him hard.

"I just wanted to drop this off and check on my stubborn patient," she teased, her lips curving into that effortless smile of hers.

He chuckled, though it sent a fresh wave of pain through his skull.

Still, he didn't care.

He reached for her, pulled her into his arms, and the second she pressed against him, something inside him just... settled.

This?

This felt right.

This was home.

And that's when he knew.

Symeria wasn't just someone he was dating.

She was someone he loved.

Someone he wanted to be with for the rest of his life.

Not just because she brought him medicine and food.

Not just because she knew what he needed without him asking.

But because of who she was.

Because of the way she moved through life: fearless, passionate, unwavering. Because of the way she loved her family, the way she fought for what she believed in, and the way she made time for what mattered.

Symeria wasn't all work and no play like he had first assumed.

She was all business, but she was also all heart.

She made time for what she loved.

And Adonis knew, right then and there, that he wanted to be one of those things.

For the first time in his life, he wasn't just thinking about the future.

He was seeing it.

And Symeria?

She was right there in it.

 Trinity Sierra Sesay

CHAPTER THIRTY-FIVE

Symeria

It *was 4:30 in the morning when Sye's phone started ringing. She could not believe someone was calling her at this time back-to-back. She thought something was wrong when she heard Adonis' voice.*

"Adonis, is everything ok? It's 4:30 in the morning," she was still sleepy and partially incoherent, but she was listening. It had been two weeks since he started feeling better from his allergy issues, so she wasn't sure what was going on.

"Yes. Everything is good. I wanted to ask you something."

"This better be good," she said. It was too early to be having a full-blown conversation. "Are you sure everything is ok?" she asked again.

"Yes, everything is fine. What I want to know is, what are you doing?"

"What am I doing?" she asked, still trying to wake up.

"Yes. I mean, I know what you're doing; you were asleep, right?"

"Yeeeessss," she said, dragging out the word.

"Ok, well, here's what I want to know. Are you…? I am…" Adonis stammered, trying to remember enough words to form a cohesive sentence, "I would like some company. I was thinking about taking a ride to the beach, and I wanted to know if you would come with me?"

"The beach?" she echoed.

"Yeah, you know, I just feel like seeing the sunrise. The last time we went, it was just great, and I just wanted to…" he stopped midsentence, *"I couldn't sleep, and I felt like this would be a great day to take a ride. Maybe go watch the sunrise and then have some breakfast in Hilton Head?"*

"Ooook," Sye said, "When do you want to go?"

"I can come pick you up in about forty-five minutes. The sunrise is about 6:30 this morning, and it takes about an hour to get there."

"OK. Let's do it. I'll be ready when you get here," she was still half asleep and sure the sound of her voice reflected this.

"Cool, I'll see you then."

She knew he had something on his mind. He had a tendency to go anywhere near water when he did. It was his refuge. This wasn't anything new. They'd done this before. In the past, when they've gotten up early and gone to the beach.

She was either staying with him or he was staying with her, and they would just get up and go. She wanted to know what was bothering him, but she also just wanted to be there for him, whatever it was.

After he picked her up, they drove towards Hilton Head. On their road trips, even if they were going to the mall or just going on a long drive, they always had a good time. They would listen to the radio, talk, or just exist in each other's space. This time was different, though. They just listened to the radio. There wasn't much talking, partly because she was still sleepy. The ride wasn't usually long, but right now, it felt like it was taking forever to get to Hilton Head and it's probably because she wanted to know what was ailing him, but she didn't want to ask.

When they pulled up to the beach, Adonis parked in general parking. There were actually a few people out here this time of the morning. They got there just at the right time. It hadn't quite hit sunrise yet but you could see the orange glow of the sun over the horizon, being hidden by the clouds. The dolphins were playing in the ocean, and the seagulls were all stretched out on the beach. It was so quiet and so serene. Adonis took her hand as they walked for a little bit. It was too chilly to put their feet in the water, so they just walked along the shoreline hand in hand. They had gotten to a certain spot near the water as it was rushing up. It kind of got a little closer to them than they expected and splashed on them. She was laughing as she tried to get away from the oncoming wave. He started laughing and running, too, and then they both just ended up in each other's arms.

She looked him in his eyes, put her hands on his face, and said as they embraced, "Adonis, I love you so much."

He smiled. She wanted him to know how much she loved him. This wasn't the first time she'd told him I loved him. They've said this to each other on several occasions, but today, she wanted him to know that whatever it was bothering him, she was here for him and wanted to support him.

"I love you too, Sye," he said, but then I felt his arms sliding from my waist down to the back of her legs, and she saw him getting on his knee. It was probably clear that she didn't quite understand what was going on, and so, as Adonis' left hand fell off of her body, his right hand took her hand and kissed it.

"Sye, I know without a shadow of a doubt that you are the woman that I can't live without and that I want to be with you for the rest of my life. I brought you here because, here on this beach, at this time and space, I feel is the closest that we could get at this point to the universe, to God and to our ancestors. It is here that I want to know, Symeria, will you marry me?"

She was totally speechless. She tried to process what she was hearing, but she just kept looking at him, kneeling in the sand as the water came closer to their little part of the shore, and at this moment, she felt that they were as close to all things pure as they probably would ever be. The sun was rising, the birds were singing, and you could hear the water as it hit the shore. She didn't realize just how many people were on the beach until he said her name again.

 Trinity Sierra Sesay

"Sye, will you marry me?" For the second time, his voice took her out of her trance, and she suddenly remembered how to breathe.

"Yes," she said, "Yes, absolutely yes, I will marry you." Then, she heard clapping from some of the bystanders on the beach. "Woohoo!" one person said. Yes, people were cheering. One runner ran by and said that was an awesome proposal. He got up off his knees and embraced her, held her, and kissed her. In his embrace, it was almost like there was no one else there. It was just them. Just them, the universe, their ancestors, and God. That's what he said and that she would never forget.

They stayed on the beach a little while longer, walked, embraced, held hands, and kissed; then, as they would normally do, they stopped by a restaurant to have breakfast before they drove back to Savannah. She could not wait to get home to show her girls this ring and to tell them that she, Symeria Hayes, was now engaged. *I said YES!!!*

The timing of her return home could not have been any more perfect. Both of her girls were up, and as she walked through the door, she heard laughter coming from the kitchen. She wasn't sure if she wanted to just spring it on them or try to make them guess, but either way, she knew it was going to be fun, and she knew her girls were going to be more than happy for her. Dash was the first one to notice her coming through the door.

"Wait a minute…I thought you were in your room asleep when I went to bed last night. Where are you coming from?" Dash asked.

"Yeah, I thought I was the last one in last night, and your car was out there when I got up. What gives?" Torrie chimed in.

"Well, um," she said, trying to stay calm and not give it away. This was one time she was really glad that she had pockets because her hands were in them, and she didn't look suspicious, "Well, um, Adonis called me this morning; he wanted to talk."

"Talk?" Dash frowned, "What time was this?"

"It was about 4:30."

"4:30!" both girls yelled.

"Yeah," she said, "It was no big deal. He wanted to go and walk on the beach at Sunrise. You know he likes water; it's his element."

Torrie lifted her cup of coffee, looking at her very suspiciously.

"Ok, well, is everything ok?" Dash asked.

"Ooh, I haven't seen a sunrise on a beach in a while," Torrie added, "I bet it was beautiful." She was still sipping her coffee.

"Yes, it was beautiful, and what made it even more beautiful is I SAID YES!"

     Trinity Sierra Sesay

She pulled her hand out of her pocket and flashed the ring in front of the girls. Both were now screaming, "Oh my gosh! Oh My Gosh!"

"Wait, tell us, how did he propose?"

"What did he do?"

"What did he say?"

The girls bombarded her with questions as she recounted the events of the morning.

"The ring is beautiful, Sye," Torrie said.

"Yeah, I love it too," she admired it again, "While we were driving back, I kept looking at it and you know, he obviously gets me because you two know that I have never been one for big or flashy and this princess cut diamond is everything. It reflects me very well."

Torrie kept holding her hand, looking at the ring almost as if she were somewhere else. She wondered if all of these were too much for her, given that she had her own relationship issues. She didn't want to ask, as she didn't want to insult her, so she changed the subject. That's what best friends do.

CHAPTER THIRTY-SIX

Amari

One thing about being a man? There's never a shortage of women when you want one.

Amari smirked, watching his bruhs execute the night's strategy flawlessly. A group of educated, successful men drinking, dancing, and throwing up hooks, which got attention. And Amari wasn't mad at it.

His boys knew better than to push him about his situation. No digging into his feelings, no "bro, let's talk" nonsense. That's counselor talk. That's for women.

He was done talking. Done overanalyzing.

Tonight was about music, drinks, and women putting their backs into it on the dance floor.

After an hour, the heat inside was getting to him, so he stepped outside for some air. And that's when he heard her voice.

He turned, and there she was. Statuesque. Effortless. Unbothered.

Dash.

Amari smirked and walked up behind her, "Dash?"

She turned. For a split second, there was a flicker of something in her expression: recognition, maybe even amusement. But then, she exhaled and said, "Oh. It's you."

Amari arched a brow. Damn.

Dash must've noticed because she took a sip of her drink and added, "I didn't mean it like that. I just wasn't expecting to see anyone I knew."

He nodded. Fair enough.

"Well, that makes two of us. I definitely didn't expect to see you here."

"It's not my usual spot," she admitted, glancing around, "Just wanted a change of scenery. Clear my head."

Amari chuckled, knowing damn well that's not why he was here.

Dash tilted her head.

"So, you came to one of the loudest spots in the city…to clear your head?"

She arched a brow, unimpressed. "Yeah, okay, Amari."

He laughed. "See, now that right there," he pointed at her face, "that side-eye, the shade? Unnecessary."

 Trinity Sierra Sesay

She grinned, but her expression stayed skeptical.

"You're here for the same reason I am," Amari said, "To not be alone."

Dash didn't argue. She just exhaled and checked her watch.

"Actually," she said, "I'm getting ready to leave."

He held out a hand to stop her, "I was just about to head out, too. Hold up, let me say bye to my bruhs."

Dash crossed her arms and watched him. Sizing him up. Then, with a slight smirk, she turned and walked off.

As they left the club together, Amari couldn't let it slide.

"So, Ms. Dash," he teased, opening the door for her, "is that what you do? Just throw nonverbal cues?" He made air quotes.

She laughed, shaking her head, "Amari, darling, when you went back to your bruhs, gave them dap, pounded them hard, laughing and looking at me? That told me they think you're going home with me tonight. That's what men do."

He smirked, "I'm not like all men, Dash."

She gave him a slow, knowing look, "Mm-hmm. So, they didn't say anything congratulatory? Like, 'yo, my man, you're a lucky bastard?'"

She arched a brow.

Amari tried not to grin. Busted.

"Maybe just a little," he admitted, holding his hands up, *"But I didn't tell them anything!"*

Dash scoffed, "Yeah. But you didn't shut it down either."

He had no defense. So, he said nothing.

"Amari," she sighed, "have a good night."

He sped up to match her pace, impressed by how fast she moved in heels. Damn, she had a presence.

"At least let me walk you to your car," he said, *"Where is it?"*

"Down the street. But I'll be fine."

"Nope, nope, nope," he said, shaking his head, "You're my wife's best friend's sister. I need to make sure you're safe."

She stopped walking.

"My wife?" she repeated, giving him a look.

Amari felt that look.

Shit.

"I thought you were getting your much-wanted divorce," she said, folding her arms, *"Why are you still calling her your wife?"*

"Well, technically, she is…"

Dash let out a dry laugh, "Right."

Then she started walking again.

Amari's stomach rumbled. He realized he hadn't eaten since lunch.

     Trinity Sierra Sesay

"You hungry?" he asked, "I'm starving. Let's grab something."

She stopped again, this time actually considering it. Her face softened, "Okay. Where?"

They ended up at a late-night diner just a block away. Dash drove.

As they settled in, Amari couldn't help but study her.

Her sharp features. Her smooth, dark skin. The way her eyes held a quiet fire.

And that smile.

Damn, that smile.

"I'm surprised you agreed to come," he said.

"Why?" she asked, unrolling her silverware.

He shrugged, "I don't know. You seem kind of…standoffish."

Dash smirked, "If you thought that, why did you ask?"

"I figured, what's the worst that could happen? You say no?" *He cleared his throat, "The real question is, why'd you say yes?"*

She looked up, her eyes locking with his.

"The truth?" she asked.

He nodded.

"I got the feeling you needed to talk," she said simply, "So I figured I'd listen."

He grinned. Damn, she was good.

"Well, it's always good talking to you," he admitted.

Dash rolled her eyes, "Uh-huh. So? Spill it. What's on your mind?"

Amari exhaled, "Honestly? Nothing specific. I just wanted some female company."

Dash scoffed.

"What?" he asked, "Did I miss something?"

She leaned back and folded her arms, "Amari, just admit it. You miss Taureen."

His jaw clenched, "What?"

"All this partying, all this hanging out, it's not you. You miss your wife."

He shook his head, "Dash, she was right to give up. I wasn't giving in."

Dash studied him for a long moment. Then, she smirked, "That's some bullshit, and you know it."

He just stared at her.

A waiter arrived, bringing their late-night orders: dessert. Neither of them had wanted anything heavy.

For a moment, they ate in silence. Just watching each other.

Then, Amari said, "Dash, what exactly are you implying?"

She cut into her pastry. Didn't even look up.

"I'm not implying anything, Amari. I'm saying it outright."

She finally met his gaze, "You miss your wife."

He scoffed, "She cheated. I'm supposed to just forgive that?"

Dash held his stare, "It's a marriage, Amari. You don't think it's worth fighting for?"

His chest tightened.

"That scenario ended," he said coolly, "when she dropped her drawers and opened her legs for another man."

Dash said nothing.

She just took another bite of her pastry.

And they ate in silence.

CHAPTER THIRTY-SEVEN

Symeria

Sye stepped onto the balcony, inhaling deeply as she gazed over the city skyline. Her engagement party. She's engaged. The words still felt surreal.

She had kissed her fair share of frogs, but here she was. It was worth it.

Leaning against the railing, she let her fingers trail over the cool metal as she soaked in the moment. Then, a voice, smooth and unexpected, broke through the quiet.

"He's a good man."

She flinched, her heart nearly leaping from her chest as she turned sharply. Jesus.

"Don't sneak up on people like that," she exhaled, placing a hand over her chest.

The man, tall, brown-skinned, with chiseled features and piercing light brown eyes, watched her closely. He hadn't moved.

"Did you say something?" she asked, still catching her breath.

He studied her for a long moment before repeating, "He's a good man. Adonis, your fiancé."

His tone was odd as if she needed reminding of who her fiancé was.

She straightened, "I know he is. Thank you." Her eyes narrowed, "How do you know him?"

The man smiled slightly as if enjoying her confusion, "Where are my manners?" He extended his hand, "I'm Alex."

She hesitated before shaking it, "Nice to meet you, Alex."

"The pleasure is mine," he replied, flashing a charming smile that didn't quite reach his eyes.

She crossed her arms, "So… how do you know Adonis?"

He took a slow sip of his drink, then said, "Let's just say he was my first."

Something about his tone made her stomach tighten.

"Your first?" Her brow furrowed, "Your first what?"

He held her gaze, "Everything."

Alex smiled, a knowing, almost nostalgic smile, before delivering the next blow.

"My first love. My first lover. My first one to get away."

The words slammed into her. Everything slowed. Her breath caught, her heart pounded, and her fingers curled into fists at her sides.

"What?" She managed, barely above a whisper.

Alex nodded as if savoring the moment, "We were young. We both knew our families wouldn't accept us, so we did what we thought was best. We ended it. Went our separate ways."

He swirled his drink absently before adding, "But we never lost touch."

A smirk. A casual shrug. And then, "You're lucky to have him."

He turned to leave, and her world tilted.

Dash and Torrie chose that exact moment to step onto the balcony, laughing about something.

Torrie's eyes trailed after Alex as he disappeared into the party. "Who was that?" she asked, grinning, "Because baby, he could get it."

Dash chuckled, then froze when she caught her expression.

"Sye?" her amusement faded, "What's wrong?"

She couldn't speak.

Dash's brows knit together, "Sye?"

"Get me out of here," she whispered.

Torrie frowned, "Wait, what?"

She turned to them, eyes pleading, "Get me out of here. Now."

Dash and Torrie exchanged confused glances, but Dash moved first, rushing back inside to grab their purses. Torrie followed her lead, steering her toward the exit.

She saw Adonis across the room, deep in conversation, laughing until he saw her.

His brows snapped together. "Sye?" his voice was soft but urgent, "Where are you going? Our guests are here."

She forced a deep breath, schooling her face. Do not make a scene. But the disgust she felt simmered beneath her skin.

"I'm out," she said flatly, "I can't do this."

His brows knit together, "What? What are you talking about?"

She scoffed, "You know exactly what I'm talking about."

He glanced between her and the girls, hoping they had an answer.

Torrie and Dash just shrugged.

"So, we're doing the denial thing now?" she laughed bitterly, "Really? That's how you want to play it?"

Silence.

Guests were watching now, the room slowly quieting. She didn't care.

     Trinity Sierra Sesay

"Sye," Adonis stepped closer, voice gentle, "Sweetheart."

She flinched at the word, at the soft way he said it, and he noticed.

He reached for her. She jerked away.

"Sye, please," his voice cracked slightly, "What am I denying? Tell me."

She stared at him, at this man she thought she knew. Did he really want her to say it?

"You want me to tell you?" her voice wavered, "Fine."

The words left her lips like poison.

"You're gay."

A sharp inhale. A murmur rippled through the crowd.

Adonis froze. His jaw tightened, "What?"

"You heard me," She glared at him, "DL. Bi-curious. Whatever the hell you want to call it."

The room went completely silent.

Adonis' face darkened, "I am not gay, Symeria. I promise you that." His voice was low, controlled, but something flickered in his eyes.

She let out a hollow laugh, "Ask your lover."

His confusion deepened, "What?"

She jabbed a finger toward the crowd, "Ask Alex. Your first love. Your first lover. He told me everything."

Something clicked in Adonis' eyes. His lips parted slightly in realization, then his expression shifted.

Adonis scanned the room. Then, he spotted Alex.

"Alex!" his voice boomed through the venue.

Alex stepped forward, hands raised in surrender. "I'm sorry, man," he said quickly, "Really. I didn't mean…"

Adonis closed his eyes, exhaling sharply before facing her again.

"Sye." He said it slowly, carefully, syllable by syllable, "Sy—mer—ia."

His voice was steady, but his chest rose and fell sharply.

He held up a hand, bracing her, "But here's the thing. My first love was a 17-year-old girl."

He paused. His voice dropped lower.

"Alexis. Alexis."

A hush fell over the room.

Dash's head snapped toward Alex, "Wait… you're transgender?"

Alex gave a small, apologetic smile, "Yes."

She blinked. Her mind raced.

Adonis turned to her, "Sye, I swear I didn't hide anything from you. Alex, Alexis, and I were together years ago in high school. He is my oldest friend. She transitioned as an adult."

Alex stepped forward, "I thought you knew. I was just joking around." His face genuinely fell, "I'm sorry. I really am."

Adonis looked at her, "I love you. I am the man you think I am."

The room was waiting for her to respond. To forgive.

But she couldn't.

It wasn't about Alex. It was about trust. It was about choice.

She turned. Walked out.

Dash and Torrie followed without hesitation.

Adonis' voice rang out behind her, "Symeria, Symeria, wait!"

She stopped short of Torrie's car and turned.

"I just…I can't," she whispered.

His face fell.

And with that, she got in the car.

And they drove away.

CHAPTER THIRTY-EIGHT

Adonis

It had been three days since Adonis spoke to Sye. The funny thing was, he hadn't tried to call her, and she hadn't tried to call him. It was like they were mutually choosing silence as if the engagement party disaster had never happened.

Standing under the scalding hot water of his shower, he let the steam surround him, but it didn't do much to clear his mind. Why didn't she fight for him? Why did she believe Alex so easily, without questioning him? The distrust stung more than he wanted to admit, but it wasn't the first time he'd felt it.

Sye's reaction triggered something he thought he had buried long ago.

Adonis clenched his jaw as a memory surfaced: the day Jewel, the woman he had planned to propose to, confessed that she had fallen in love with someone else.

And not just anyone; his father.

He could still hear her voice, wavering but firm, "I never meant for it to happen, Adonis, but I can't lie to you. Your father... he just understands me in ways you never could."

His own father.

The man who raised him, the man who taught him everything he knew about life, business, and discipline, the man who looked him in the eye and said nothing as he took everything from him.

Adonis exhaled sharply, shaking his head to clear the thought. It had been years, but betrayal like that doesn't just disappear. And maybe that's why Sye's reaction cut so deep. Because it felt like déjà vu. Another person he loved walking away without even considering that he was telling the truth.

Maybe this is just my fate, he thought bitterly. Women don't trust me. They love me, but they don't trust me.

The water turned lukewarm, dragging him back to the present. He turned off the shower, dried off, and got dressed. Normally, he took pride in his appearance, but today, his reflection irritated him. He felt like a fool, dressed well, running a business, financially stable, checking every damn box... and yet, still standing in the same spot, wondering if the woman he loved would ever see him clearly.

Maybe the bigger question wasn't why she hadn't called. Maybe it was why he hadn't either.

⸻⸘⸻

       Trinity Sierra Sesay

The coffee shop was quiet, except for the hum of conversation around them. Adonis stirred his drink absently, his mind stuck in the silence.

Three days.
Three days since the engagement party.
Three days since Sye walked out.
Three days where neither of them had reached out.

Across from him, Alex exhaled and leaned forward, "Look, man… I know I already said it a hundred times, but I really am sorry. I didn't mean to cause all that drama."

Adonis let out a short laugh, shaking his head, "I know you didn't, Alex. That's not even the point."

Alex frowned, "Then what *is* the point?"

Adonis set down his spoon, rubbing a hand over his jaw. He was exhausted, "The point is how easy it was for her to believe you. No questions. No doubt. Just… *gone*."

Alex tilted his head, "That really got to you, huh?"

Adonis scoffed, "Wouldn't it get to you? I mean, damn, Alex. We've been together for months. We've built something real. And she just… walked away. Like it was that simple." He let out a slow exhale, forcing himself to stay calm, "You want to know what that reminded me of?"

Alex was already nodding, "Jewel."

"Damn right," Adonis let out a bitter laugh, shaking his head, "You remember how she ended things? Just *decided* one day that we were done. No conversation. No warning. And when I finally got her to talk, you know what she said?" He looked at Alex, his voice dropping into a mockery of Jewel's cold, detached tone: *'You were just trying too hard, and it made you look weak."*

Alex winced, "Man, I hated when she said that."

"So did I," Adonis's fingers curled into a fist on the table, "And now? Here I am again. Different woman, different situation, but the same damn feeling." He let out a slow exhale, "Sye walked away from me just like Jewel did, and I had no say in it, but one thing that is different: I am not weak, and I am not chasing after her."

Alex was quiet for a moment, watching him closely. Then he asked, "But why do you think she reacted so strongly?"

Adonis frowned, "What do you mean?"

"I mean, yeah, it was a messed-up situation. But she didn't even stay to talk about it. That wasn't just anger, bro. That was something deeper."

Adonis sighed, rubbing a hand over his face, "So what? You're saying this wasn't about me?"

Alex shrugged, "I'm saying… what if it wasn't? What if this wasn't even about the perception of lying but something else?"

Adonis sat back, staring at him.

For the first time in three days, Adonis wasn't just angry.

For the first time, he wondered if Sye had been just as triggered as he was.

 Trinity Sierra Sesay

CHAPTER THIRTY-NINE

Dash

Dash came downstairs, rubbing her temples. She hadn't even made it to the fridge when she saw her sister sitting at the table, staring into her untouched coffee.

Three days. That's how long it had been since the engagement party fell apart.

Three days of silence. No calls. No texts. No fight. And Dash was sick of it.

"Are you going to tell me the truth now?" she asked, pouring her juice.

Sye barely looked up, "Not really."

Dash sighed, "Oh, we're playing this game again."

"Symeria, this is me you're talking to, me, your sister. You do remember that, right?" She folded her arms, pinning Sye with a look, "I know you. And right now, I know you're full of shit."

Sye exhaled, pressing a palm against her forehead.

Dash kept going.

"You walked out of your engagement party for a good reason, not mad at that, but three days later? Nothing? No call? No text? Neither of you?"

She shook her head, "What the hell kind of love is that?"

Silence.

Dash leaned against the counter, watching Sye. Her sister had shut down, and that was the real problem. The Symeria she knew wasn't a coward. She wasn't afraid of confrontation. But this? This wasn't about the fight at the party.

This was about something else.

Sye let out a breath and finally spoke.

"I haven't called him because I don't know what to say."

Dash folded her arms, "Here we go."

"The thing is," Sye continued, looking at Dash for the first time, "if I wasn't willing to fight for him, and he isn't fighting for me, what does that say about us?"

Dash didn't answer.

"I mean, think about it, we both did the same thing," Sye said, "We shut down." She let out a small, bitter laugh, "How do you build a future with someone when neither of you knows how to fight for it?"

Dash sighed, "You're talking in circles, Sye. What are you really scared of?"

Sye opened her mouth, then shut it again.

Dash's eyes narrowed. That hesitation? That was it.

"Sye," Dash pressed, "why were you still mad after Alex explained everything? You didn't even give Adonis a chance to talk. Why?"

Sye's jaw clenched.

"I believed him too fast," she admitted. Her voice was tight, her hands curled around her coffee mug, "I didn't ask questions. I didn't push back. Alex said it, and I believed it."

Dash leaned forward, "And why do you think that is?"

Sye let out a hollow laugh, "Because I've been here before."

Dash said nothing. There it was.

Sye stared down at her coffee, her fingers absently tracing the rim.

"I thought I'd moved on. I thought I was past it. But when Alex said what he said, it was like…" She exhaled sharply, "It was like I was watching it happen again."

Dash frowned.

"Sye, what are you talking about?"

Sye swallowed. Her voice was barely a whisper.

"I didn't see it coming, Dash. Last time… I didn't see it coming."

Dash stayed quiet.

"One day, I thought everything was fine. We were living our lives happy, at least, I thought we were." Sye let out a bitter laugh, "Lindsey and I would talk about *our* future, the house, the kids, the businesses, everything. The thing is that we never stopped talking. Even after the accident, we were still talking. Still planning."

She exhaled sharply, her fingers tightening around the mug, "But in one short moment, the conversation changed. And then everything changed. Our lives together became his life, and just like that, I was no longer a part of it. He thought about it. He made the decision. He controlled the narrative. And his decision impacted my life."

Sye shook her head, her voice quieter but no less sharp, "And what did I get to do? What part did I play? Accept it. Accept *his* decision and say goodbye."

Dash's jaw tightened.

Sye shook her head, her grip tightening around the mug, "I didn't even get a chance to fight for it. It was already over."

Dash exhaled slowly.

Sye let out a breath, shaky this time, "So when Alex said what he said and told me his story, my first instinct wasn't to ask. It was to run. Because I thought, this time, I get to decide. This time, I walk away, I get to make the decision, and I get to control the narrative."

Dash's brows pulled together, "But what if it wasn't the same?"

Sye exhaled sharply, "What if it was?"

A beat of silence.

"And what if it wasn't?" Dash asked again, softer this time.

Sye nodded slowly.

Dash tapped her fingers against the table, processing.

"So… what now?" she finally asked.

Sye looked away.

"I don't know."

Dash studied her for a long moment.

Then, gently, she said, "Sye… Adonis is still here."

Sye's breath hitched.

"He hasn't left. He hasn't walked away. You did."

The words hit hard, but Dash didn't let up.

"You're not that woman anymore, Sye. The one who just gets left behind. But if you don't pick up that phone, if you don't fight for this, then you're choosing to let him go."

Sye swallowed.

"So," Dash said, tilting her head, "what are you going to do about it?"

CHAPTER FORTY

Amari

Amari sat in the counselor's office, noticing the quietness of the room when he focused on the patterned clicks coming from the wall clock. The clock was a rather large one, sprayed in a distressed vintage green. He hadn't noticed it in previous visits or how loud the second hand ticked as it moved. Even though there were two people sitting in the room, it felt empty, cold, stoic.

"Amari," Dr. Apara's voice cut through the silence, "I must admit that I was a bit surprised to see that on your own you scheduled an appointment to see me. How can I help you?"

It felt strange being in this office without Taureen as if something about this moment made it more real.

"Doc, look, listen to me, okay? Yes, I know what I said, and I truly meant it when I said that I wanted a divorce... at least, I meant it at the time. I think I still mean it..." he exhaled heavily, "But that's not my issue."

He adjusted his body in the chair, uncomfortable under the weight of his own thoughts, "My issue is this. All this time, she fought for us. She begged for counseling. She begged for a second chance. Now, just like that, she's agreeing with me? Divorce is the best option? That's it?" He shook his head, lips pressed together, "Doesn't that say something to you? Something isn't right. I think she's back with her lover."

"You think she's moved on?" Dr. Apara's tone was neutral and unreadable.

Amari scoffed, "What else would explain it? One minute, she's begging to make things work. The next, she's agreeing with me? I don't buy it. She's done fighting because she found someone else. She just needed time to line it up."

"Amari…" the doctor crossed her legs, resting a notepad on her knee, "Tell me something, how long were you expecting her to fight for you?"

Amari frowned, "What do you mean?"

"I mean exactly what I said. You've spent the last six months shutting her out. You controlled the narrative. You called the shots. You told her this marriage was over. And when she tried to repair things, you dismissed her. You dismissed me. You dismissed this entire process."

She leaned forward slightly, "So I ask again, how long were you expecting her to fight for you before she had enough? A year? A lifetime? Or just long enough to make you feel like you were still in control?"

Amari clenched his jaw. He didn't like the way she said that. He didn't like the way it sounded like the truth.

"She wanted to fix things," he muttered, "Then she just… gave up."

"No, Amari. She accepted," Dr. Apara's voice was calm and deliberate, "She accepted that you weren't going to change your mind. She accepted that you were done. But you never considered that acceptance wasn't the same as moving on."

The weight of her words sank into his chest.

For six months, he had all the power: rejecting her, dismissing her, making her beg. He'd assumed that as long as he held the door open, she'd always be standing on the other side, knocking.

But now? The door was closed.

And he hadn't been the one to close it.

Dr. Apara let the silence stretch between them before speaking again.

"You thought you were in control. Now that you're not, you don't know what to do with it."

Amari exhaled sharply, looking down at his hands.

For the first time in six months, he didn't have an answer.

Finally, he lifted his eyes, "What do I do now, doc?"

CHAPTER FORTY-ONE

The Duo

"This is some real high school mess," Dash muttered, giving Torrie a hard side-eye as they walked up to Adonis' office building.

"I know, but let's be real, if we don't step in, neither of them will."

Dash sucked her teeth, "And what if this backfires? Then we got two pissed-off people, one of whom we live with."

Torrie smirked, "Both, that's why we make sure it doesn't."

Dash exhaled sharply, "If this blows up, I'm telling Sye it was all your idea."

Torrie just laughed and pulled open the office door.

The inside of the building was nothing like its bland exterior. It had a sleek, modern feel: deep green walls, polished wood panels, and black leather furniture. The place was busy but calm, the energy productive but not chaotic.

Dash barely had time to admire the space when a familiar voice called from above.

"Torrie? Dash?"

They both looked up to see Adonis standing at the top of the staircase, staring down at them with a mix of curiosity and suspicion.

He started down the stairs, "This is a surprise."

Dash smirked, "That's the idea."

By the time he reached them, Adonis' expression had shifted from curiosity to guarded concern, "What's going on? Is Sye okay?"

"She's fine," Dash said, "but you? Not so much."

Adonis' eyes narrowed, "What?"

Torrie crossed her arms, "How long has it been now? Over a week? No calls. No texts. Not a single attempt from either of you to fix this?"

Adonis exhaled, "She hasn't reached out either."

Dash scoffed, "And that's the game y'all are playing? Who can hold out the longest?"

Adonis shrugged, "I took her walking away as an answer."

Torrie rolled her eyes, "No, you took it as an excuse."

Adonis' jaw tightened, but he said nothing.

Dash shook her head, "Let's cut the BS. You love her. She loves you. But y'all both got too much damn pride to say it first."

Adonis folded his arms, "What do you want me to do? Go beg?"

Torrie gave him a look, "Nobody said beg. But if you really think this is just about what happened at the party, you're not as smart as I thought."

Adonis frowned, "She walked away."

"And you let her," Dash countered.

His lips parted slightly, but he didn't speak.

Torrie tilted her head, "Tell me something, Adonis. Why do you think she reacted so strongly?"

He sighed, "Because she thought I lied."

Dash gave him a knowing look, "Or... what if this wasn't even about you lying?"

Adonis rubbed his chin, considering that for the first time.

Torrie leaned in, "You ever thought about what walking away means to her? Why that was her instinct?"

Adonis exhaled slowly.

Dash softened her tone, "Look, we're not saying she was right. But you know she's been through some real stuff, just like you have. Maybe this ain't just about y'all being stubborn. Maybe there's something deeper going on here."

Adonis' face was unreadable, but for the first time, he looked unsure.

Torrie pressed on, "You keep saying she walked away. But ask yourself this: did she really? Or did you?

Something flickered in Adonis' expression. His lips pressed into a tight line.

Dash tilted her head, "Doesn't feel good, does it?"

Silence stretched between them.

Finally, Adonis let out a slow breath and nodded, "Alright."

Torrie and Dash exchanged glances.

"What are you suggesting?" Adonis asked.

"Can we just talk?" Torrie asked, "After all, we are your friends now, too."

⁂

"So, yeah... it's a mess," Adonis said, pushing his half-empty coffee cup around the table. He looked up at Torrie and Dash, a flicker of pain still raw in his eyes, "You know Jewel... Jewel and I, we were... we were serious."

Dash leaned forward, her brow furrowed, "We know *of* her, Adonis. Sye's mentioned her. But not... this."

"Me neither," Adonis said, a bitter laugh escaping him, "Me neither. But, see, that's the thing. She left. For... for my dad."

Torrie's eyes widened, "Your *dad*? Seriously?"

"Dead serious. I know, right? It's like something out of a trashy soap opera," Adonis ran a hand through his hair, the gesture conveying years of frustration. "It started... well, it started with a traffic thing. A minor fender-bender or maybe a ticket. Dad, being a cop, helped her out. Nothing major, just... you know, the usual 'I'll see what I can do' stuff."

"Okay," Dash said, her gaze steady, "Go on."

"She took him for coffee as a thank you. It wasn't weird, right? We were all in each other's lives. But then, they started talking. She was having doubts about us, about me. And Dad... Dad... he listened. He gave her the kind of... I don't know, the kind of reassurance I guess she wasn't getting from me. He was calm, collected, the 'strong, silent type' thing she always said she admired."

Torrie shook her head slightly. "And she just... switched? Just like that?"

"Pretty much. She said... she said I was too... intense. That I was trying too hard. That I was suffocating her. That Dad, he just *understood* her in a way I never could. It wasn't some grand, malicious plan. It just... happened. They just clicked, she said. I was the one who was the problem. She said I was weak because I tried to fix it. I begged, I pleaded, and I tried to show her I could change.

I was a mess, and she said it proved her point," Adonis paused, swallowing hard.

"She said I made myself look weak by trying to get her back. That I should have just... let her go. That if I had been more like my dad, more stoic, more... in control, maybe she would have stayed. But I loved her! I couldn't just stand by and watch her walk away. I thought fighting for her would show her how much I cared."

Dash reached across the table and placed her hand on his arm. "And your dad?" she asked quietly, "How's he..."

"He's... he's happy. Or at least, he seems to be. He's always been distant, you know? Always the cop, always the 'tough guy.' I guess he finally found someone who appreciates that. And me? I'm just... I was left just trying to figure out how to pick up the pieces. I mean, really, how do you compete with your own father? How do you unlearn everything you thought you knew about love and relationships?" Adonis sighed, the weight of his words settling heavily in the air, "It's not just the betrayal, it's the... the humiliation. The feeling that I wasn't enough. That I was too much and not enough, all at the same time."

Torrie looked at Dash, a silent question passing between them. It was clear Adonis and Symeria needed to talk. Real Talk.

CHAPTER FORTY-TWO

Taureen

Taureen had expected this day to come, what she hadn't expected was that Amari would be the one to initiate it. He had been the one to say counseling was a waste of time. He had insisted there was nothing left to discuss. So why now?

She wasn't sure what he had to say, but if the last six months had taught her anything, it was that her tolerance had limits.

She was done being disrespected.

"Taureen," he said, his tone softer than usual.

She lifted an eyebrow, "Amari." The sharpness in her voice was deliberate. She wasn't here to make this easy.

Amari exhaled heavily. There was something different about her today. The woman sitting across from him wasn't the one who had been desperately trying to make this marriage work. She was steady. Resolved. He wasn't sure how to feel about that.

"Torrie, look," he started, shifting forward in his chair, "I was angry. And I was hurt. I'm still hurt. But I know I was wrong for how I treated you. I…" he swallowed hard, "I'm apologizing. And I'm asking for your forgiveness."

Torrie just looked at him. Then, slowly, she turned to Dr. Apara.

"Taureen," the counselor prompted gently, "how do you feel about what Amari just said?"

Torrie took in a slow breath before shifting her gaze back to him. She studied him. The furrow in his brow, the slight downturn of his lips; he wasn't faking this. He meant it.

And yet…

"I want to say I'm happy you've finally come to your senses," she said, "But I'm not."

Amari blinked, stunned, "What?"

She lifted a hand, "Let me finish."

Dr. Apara nodded at Amari, reminding him it was her turn to speak.

"The truth is," Torrie continued, her voice steady, "I understand that you were hurting. But the way you chose to handle that? The way you spoke to me, the way you degraded me over and over, that wasn't just about pain. That was about punishment. You wanted me to hurt. You wanted me to feel as bad as you did." She took a shaky breath, "And you succeeded."

The room was thick with silence.

"I never thought you would be that person, Amari," she said, softer now, "But you were. And now I don't know if I'll ever get past that."

She saw the flicker of panic in his eyes before he tried to mask it.

"I love you," she admitted, "I do. That won't change. But I agree with you now. Maybe a divorce really is what's best."

Amari's face fell.

"You see that, Doc?" his voice rose in frustration as he turned toward Dr. Apara, "I told you! She doesn't want me; she wants him. That's why she's so quick to give up." He threw a hand in the air, "She's in love with that guy."

Torrie didn't react. She just watched him.

Watched him spiral.
Watched him make excuses.
Watched him cling to the same tired narrative that let him avoid facing himself.

And suddenly, everything was clear.

"You know, Amari," she said, her voice eerily calm, "if I wasn't sure about my decision before, I am now."

She stood up.

"We're done."

Amari's mouth opened… and then closed.

Dr. Apara remained quiet, observing the moment.

Torrie adjusted her purse on her shoulder and pulled out a white envelope. She set it down in front of Amari.

He frowned and reached for it. The paper tore as he ripped it open. A metallic clink followed.

Their wedding rings hit the floor.

Amari stared at them before his eyes darted to the papers in his hands. Petition for Dissolution of Marriage.

Uncontested. Signed.

Torrie had left him nothing to fight.

Amari's hands trembled slightly as he skimmed the pages.

Torrie exhaled and turned to Dr. Apara, "Thank you for your time."

Then, without another word, she walked out.

And for the first time since this all started, she felt free.

CHAPTER FORTY-THREE

Symeria

The museum smelled like aged wood and oil paints, and something ancient, like history itself, had been woven into the walls.

Symeria moved slowly through the exhibit, her heels clicking softly against the polished floors as she studied the artifacts.

The new collection featured artwork from West African countries, a stunning mix of Mende fertility figures, Cameroonian royal masks, and carved wooden Sankofa birds, all symbolizing creation, memory, and the importance of looking back to move forward.

She had come here with Torrie and Dash, eager to immerse herself in something beyond her own emotions.

But now, standing before a Mende fertility sculpture, she found herself lost in thought.

The statue was carved from dark wood, a regal figure with delicate curves, arms stretched outward as if offering something unseen.

According to the plaque, it represented renewal. Rebirth. A second chance.

Symeria traced the words with her eyes.

"A second chance."

The phrase sat heavy in her chest.

She exhaled, shaking her head. Maybe this was a mistake. Maybe I shouldn't have come.

And then…

A voice behind her. Deep. Familiar. Too familiar.

"Déjà vu."

Symeria froze.

"Last time we were in a museum together," the voice continued, softer now, closer, *"you spent twenty minutes debating the meaning of a single brushstroke."*

Symeria turned, already knowing who it was before she saw him.

Adonis.

He stood just a few feet away, dressed in a fitted black sweater and dark jeans, hands in his pockets.

     Trinity Sierra Sesay

The sight of him made something inside her tighten, a feeling she wasn't ready for.

Symeria: *"And I was right."*

A smirk tugged at the corner of Adonis's mouth. *"Debatable."*

She tried to ignore the way his voice wrapped around her like a memory, warm and unsettling all at once.

Adonis (gesturing to the statue): *"And this one? What's the verdict?"*

Symeria turned back to the display.

Symeria (quietly): *"It's about creation. Rebirth. Starting again."*

The words sat heavy between them.

A long pause.

Adonis: "Maybe that's a sign."

She glanced at him, really looking at him this time.

The sharp cut of his jaw. The familiar crease between his brows, the one that only appeared when he was thinking too hard.

Symeria let out a slow breath.

Symeria: "Or maybe it's just a statue."

Adonis chuckled softly, shaking his head, "Maybe."

Another pause.

Longer this time.

He looked like he wanted to say something else, but didn't.

And maybe that was for the best.

Symeria swallowed, breaking the silence first.

Symeria: *"So… what brings you here?"*

Adonis (shrugging, glancing toward Dash and Torrie): "Some friends invited me."

Symeria followed his gaze, immediately spotting Dash and Torrie pretending to study a textile display with way too much enthusiasm.

She let out a slow exhale, shaking her head, "Of course, they did."

"Well, I guess that makes two of us." She said as she looked at them with squinted eyes.

Another lingering moment.

Symeria felt Dash and Torrie watching from across the room, pretending to be interested in a textile display.

She sighed.

"This is weird, isn't it?" Sye said sheepishly.

Adonis nodded, "A little."

And then, he did something she didn't expect.

     Trinity Sierra Sesay

He smiled. Not the guarded, careful kind, but the real kind. The kind that made her chest ache.

Adonis: "The coffee shop down the block is still there."

She blinked, caught off guard.

Adonis (softly): "You want to go? Just for coffee. No expectations."

The weight of the moment settled between them.

Symeria hesitated, searching his face.

There was no pressure in his expression, no demand, just an open door.

Her heart beat against her ribs.

Could she do this?

Did she want to?

Symeria took one last look at the statue, the symbol of rebirth, renewal, and a second chance.

Then, slowly, she nodded.

Symeria: *"Yeah. Let's go."*

CHAPTER FORTY-FOUR

The Couple

Three months later.

Symeria sat across from Adonis in the softly lit office, her hands resting in her lap. The walls were lined with bookshelves, a few serene paintings, and a tall window letting in the early spring light. Dr. Nyland, calm as ever, observed them from her chair with an encouraging expression.

"So," the therapist said, glancing at them both, "it's been three months since you made the decision to work through things. How do you feel about where you are now?"

Symeria hesitated before answering. She glanced at Adonis, then back at Dr. Nyland, "I think… we're learning how to stay when it's uncomfortable. How to have hard conversations without assuming the worst."

Adonis nodded, his fingers lightly drumming against his knee, "Yeah. We're unlearning some things, and that's not easy. But it's necessary."

Dr. Nyland smiled, "That's progress."

Symeria exhaled, rolling her shoulders, "It's not always easy."

Adonis let out a short laugh, "Understatement of the year."

Symeria shot him a look, but a smirk played at the corner of her lips.

Dr. Nyland leaned forward, "You've both done a lot of work in a short amount of time. But tell me, what feels different now?"

Symeria took a moment before speaking, "I'm not waiting for the rug to be pulled from under me. I'm not assuming that if something goes wrong, it means everything is falling apart."

Adonis nodded, "And I'm learning that I don't have to fix everything. That showing up, really showing up, matters more than trying to control the outcome."

Dr. Nyland studied them, "That's the thing about relationships. They aren't just about love. They're about trust. About knowing that if one of you stumbles, the other won't just walk away."

Symeria met Adonis's gaze. He held it.

Dr. Nyland smiled at their silent exchange, "You two have something worth holding onto. And it looks like you're finally learning how to hold on, even when it would be easier to let go."

Symeria let out a slow, relieved sigh.

Adonis reached for her hand, and this time, she didn't pull away.

Dr. Nyland stood, walking toward her desk, "That's all for today, but I'd like to see you both next month for a check-in."

They both nodded, standing as well.

As they walked out of the office, Symeria squeezed Adonis's hand.

"You hungry?" she asked.

Adonis smirked, "Always."

"Good," I said, "I'm driving. No complaints."

Adonis chuckled, shaking his head, "I'll try my best."

They walked down the hallway together, side by side.

Not perfect. Not fully healed.

But no longer with goodbye being their only option.

The End

EPILOGUE

And Then…

Dash had fully expected Sye and Torrie to grill her before she left the party.

But to her relief (and mild disappointment), they were too wrapped up in the celebration to notice when she slipped out.

The moment she stepped into the waiting Lyft, she felt her pulse pick up.

By the time she reached the hotel, anticipation coiled tightly in her stomach.

She thanked the driver, stepped out, and strode through the glass doors.

The concierge barely looked up as she approached the desk.

"Eleventh floor," Dash murmured.

The woman nodded toward the elevators.

Dash's heels clicked against the marble as she made her way down the empty hall, stopping in front of room 1107.

She took a deep breath.

Then, she knocked lightly.

The door swung open almost immediately.

A familiar warmth filled the space between them.

"I missed you," a deep voice said.

Dash looked up, eyes locking onto his.

Alex.

She exhaled sharply, stepping into his embrace.

"Me too," she whispered against his lips.

The kiss that followed was slow, familiar.

Intentional.

Dash reached back, grabbing the door handle.

She slipped the "Do Not Disturb" sign in place and then shut the door behind her.

ABOUT THE AUTHOR

Trinity Sierra Sesay writes emotionally rich, character-driven stories that explore love, loss, healing, and the power of choosing yourself. With a gift for capturing the quiet moments that define human connection, her work invites readers to sit with the complicated parts of life and find beauty in them. *When Goodbye Is All You Have* is a testament to her ability to blend raw vulnerability with grounded strength, offering readers stories that resonate long after the final page.

www.ingramcontent.com/pod-product-compliance
Lightning Source LLC
Chambersburg PA
CBHW020412110726
47899CB00006B/1954